Mills & Boon Classics

A chance to read and collect some of the best-loved novels
from Mills & Boon – the world's largest publisher of
romantic fiction.

Every month, four titles by favourite Mills & Boon authors
will be re-published in the *Classics* series.

A list of other titles in the *Classics* series can be found at the
end of this book.

Mary Burchell

A SONG BEGINS

MILLS & BOON LIMITED
LONDON · TORONTO

First published 1965
Australian copyright 1980
Philippine copyright 1980
This edition 1980

This edition © Mary Burchell 1980

ISBN 0 263 73297 5

Set in Monotype Plantin 10 on 12 pt.

Made and printed in Great Britain by
Richard Clay (The Chaucer Press), Ltd.,
Bungay, Suffolk

CHAPTER I

IT was raining, but she was not aware of it. People passed her, but she did not see them. For, as she climbed the steep hill to the small house at the top where she lived, Anthea Benton walked in a world of her own.

There had been nothing to tell her that this day would not be like any other day. She had gone to her singing lesson that afternoon expecting it to be like any other singing lesson. Absorbing, fascinating, challenging — but just a singing lesson.

And then, at the end, Miss Sharon — her strict, somewhat waspish, utterly dedicated teacher — had said, "Sit down, Anthea. I have something serious to say to you."

She had sat down, impressed by Miss Sharon's air, her heart beating suddenly lest she were going to be told that, on reflection, her teacher thought it a waste of time for her to go on with her studies. (From which it will be seen that Anthea had a nice sense of modesty and no delusions of grandeur.) Possibly it was because of this innate humility of Anthea's that Miss Sharon — a cautious and critical woman — allowed herself to continue:

"I have never said this to any pupil before, Anthea, and I doubt if I shall ever have reason to say it again. But of all those who have passed through my hands — and heaven knows they have been a motley lot —" she added acidly, "you are the only one to convince me that you are worthy of a professional career."

5

"Why – why, thank you." Anthea gave a small gasp of pleasure and relief, for Miss Sharon had been sparing with her praise up to now. "But that's always been my intention, you know. Not just to be a girl who takes singing lessons. I mean to be a singer."

Miss Sharon threw up her hands in what she believed to be a continental manner and emitted a short, contemptuous laugh.

"So do they all," she said. "So do they all. They come here full of confidence, twittering or bellowing, simpering or soulful, many unable to read a note of music, but all convinced that the world is waiting, open-mouthed, to hear them. And not one of them really has the talent, inspiration, dedication, grit, health or sheer guts to make the genuine article."

"And – you think I have?" Suddenly it was difficult to breathe.

"I know you have," retorted Miss Sharon sharply. "But remember, we can take no credit for our gifts. It's what we do with them that matters. And God gave you" – she made it sound almost like a personal matter – "the rarest of all singing gifts : a completely even scale and a natural placement."

"You mean it – it doesn't often happen?"

"Hardly ever. And nine out of ten of the people to whom it does happen waste the gift. Either because they haven't the wit or the luck to recognise it, or they are too lazy to develop it, or they want to marry some young man or have a good time or one of the other half-dozen things that are fatal to a career. I hope" – Miss Sharon fixed her with a singularly stern glance – "that you don't intend to fall into any of those errors. It would be wasting your talents in the biblical sense of the term."

"Yes, Miss Sharon. I mean – no, Miss Sharon." Anthea

had felt almost like a child before this intimidating view of her gifts. And she added fervently, "I promise to go on working hard with you —"

"No," interrupted Miss Sharon. "That's what I'm coming to, Anthea. Not with me. You are ready for wider horizons now."

"But, Miss Sharon, you're such a good teacher!"

"Yes. I'm a good, sound, drudging teacher," agreed Miss Sharon, who was a realist. "I've taught you all I can. You needed singularly little except careful guidance in this early stage. But I can't open the great professional world of musical art for you. No one in this small provincial town can do that. The next stage is not only a question of what you learn at your lessons, in the studio. You have to hear the great, and analyse what *makes* them great, you have to widen your musical experience, live your art as well as study it academically. The perfect diamond has many facets," Miss Sharon explained, in a sudden flight of fancy. "It's almost never that the same hand cuts them all. The time has come, much sooner than we ever imagined, for you to go to London."

Anthea looked grave.

"There's not much money in our household since my father's illness," she said frankly. "He's only just back at work. And my brother's still at school. I don't think they could —"

"Go home and explain to them what I have told you," interrupted Miss Sharon with a touch of ruthlessness. "They may have to make sacrifices now. The families of artists usually have to. But when you're famous, they'll think it was worth it."

When you're famous! As she walked homeward, those incredible words rang in Anthea's ears like a chime of bells. When you're famous —

7

With an extravagance beyond anything her teacher had expressed, suddenly Anthea's imagination began to blossom. Concert halls loomed before her, opera houses took shape in front of her, audiences applauded her, managers sought her, conductors praised her.

When you're famous!

"Mother, Mother –" Anthea rushed into the house, and through to the large stone-flagged kitchen where Mrs. Benton was just taking a batch of bread from the oven.

"What's the matter?" Her mother looked up expectantly.

"Mum," – Anthea came and hugged her suddenly – "did you ever *really* think I might be famous?"

"Of course," replied her mother coolly, as she tested the crispness of a crusty loaf with an expert finger. "Just you work hard with Miss Sharon, and one of these days –"

"Mother," said Anthea a little unsteadily, "it *is* one of these days – now. Miss Sharon says it's time I went to London – that I need wider horizons."

"Wider horizons?" Mrs. Benton repeated the words in an odd, uncertain tone. The tone of one who believes in miracles but also knows the ruthless demands of daily life. "That's going to mean a lot of money, isn't it?"

Anthea nodded, wordlessly.

"Your father's back at work now, of course." The words came out slowly, consideringly.

"And I might get a part-time job in London –"

"And Roland's in his last year at school –"

"And I wouldn't mind *how* frugally I lived –"

They were tossing the bright ball of hope backwards and forwards between them, and they looked curiously alike, mother and daughter, as they stood either side of the kitchen table, with the loaves of delicious-smelling bread between them.

In a strange way, they were *like* the bread. Basic, wholesome, intensely real. Both were tall and straight, both had the same wide brown eyes and the same fine, up-springing fair hair, though the older woman's had some grey in it now. But, above all, they both had that indefinable glow of inner warmth and vitality at which the less fortunate will always seek to warm their hands.

"We'll manage somehow," Mrs. Benton said resolutely. "There's always a way. Go and see who that is, dear –" as a ring at the front door bell interrupted their conversation.

"Do you really mean, Mother –" Anthea paused and looked back eagerly from the doorway.

"I mean that, short of some disaster, I'll get you to London," replied her mother, setting her lips in a firm line. "Answer the door, Anthea –" as the ring was repeated with some urgency.

It was strange how certain phrases seemed to start up in Anthea's consciousness that afternoon, with a meaning out of all proportion to their natural context.

"Short of some disaster –" The words gave her a queer premonitory chill, so that her heart began to beat fast, as though with some pre-knowledge, even before she snatched open the front door.

And then she knew, immediately, when she saw who was standing outside. It was Neil Prentiss, the younger of the two brothers who owned the mills where her father was a floor manager, and his good-looking face was grave and concerned.

"Miss Benton, is your mother in?"

"Yes," said Anthea. "What is it? It's – Father, isn't it?"

"I'm afraid so. But it may not be too serious." He made a quick gesture of reassurance. "He collapsed at work half an hour ago, and we've had to get him into hospital again. Tell your mother I have the car here and –"

But Mrs. Benton was already at the door, white but calm.

"All right, Mr. Prentiss." She was untying her apron and smoothing her hair. "Come in, will you? I'll get a coat."

He came in and through to the kitchen, because Anthea was too dazed to take him anywhere else. But, although she offered him a seat, he chose to stand, his tall figure throwing a long shadow in the firelight.

She tried to make some sort of conversation, but few words came. And he — perhaps equally at a loss — said:

"I'm glad you were home. It makes it easier for your mother. Had you just come in from work?"

She shook her head.

"From my singing lesson," she said heavily.

"Oh, you sing?" He seemed interested, or at least contrived to sound as though he were. "Yes, you look as though you might."

"How do you know?" She still forced herself to make perfunctory conversation. "Do you sing yourself?"

"No." He laughed. "Not a note. But I'm passionately interested. That's why Prentiss's are one of the local firms backing this T.V. competition."

"Oh," said Anthea politely. And then her mother came back, and she and Neil Prentiss went off together and Anthea was alone.

It is hard to be alone when one's hopes are at zero. It would not have been so hard, Anthea thought, if she had not just been beguiled by the most dazzling, golden dreams.

When you're famous —

But those words were futile now. One must pull one's weight in a household threatened by disaster. Why should she, of them all, expect good fortune on a silver plate? All that talk about the families of artists having to make sacrifices! Her father was ill, her mother anxious, her brother

10

too young to share the burden.

If any sacrifices were to be made, it was *she* who would have to make them. The sacrifice of those glorious illusions which had irradiated one single hour.

Presently her brother, Roland, came in. He was a hardworking, uninhibited boy, with a near-genius for maths which never failed to astound his sister, to whom figures were a mystery and a menace.

She told him, as unsensationally as possible, about their father's collapse, and was glad that he took it quietly.

"Poor Mum! It's so worrying for her," he exclaimed. "How I wish I were a year or two older. It's tough on her having to shoulder all the worry. Did you know they actually had to raise a bit on Dad's life insurance during his recent illness?"

"No!" Anthea was aghast. "How do you know?"

"Dad told me himself. I don't think he quite meant to. But it was when Mr. Carew said I had a good chance of a scholarship to London University. Dad was terribly pleased, but said he ought to warn me that they wouldn't be able to supplement things much, as he'd even had to raise something on his life insurance."

"I wish they'd told *me*!" Anthea said.

"I suppose they didn't want you to start worrying until your training was complete. After all" – Roland grinned at her – "you're the white hope of this family, aren't you? When you're pulling in the crowds at Covent Garden, we'll all be on velvet."

"Oh, Rollie –" in her distress, the old, childish name slipped out – "that's just a dream! I don't think any of us ever realised what the training of a professional singer means in money and time. Miss Sharon told me only today" – her voice shook slightly – "that it was time I went to London. What do you suppose *that* would cost? And

11

how could I take it, even if the parents offered me money?"

There was a long silence, during which Roland cleared his throat sympathetically once or twice. Then suddenly he said,

"Why don't you go in for this T.V. competition they're organising at the Town Hall?"

"What competition?"

"Something that's being financed partly by the new T.V. station in this area, and partly by some of the big local firms—Prentiss's among them, I believe."

"Why," exclaimed Anthea, " he *said* something about it, and I was too – Rollie, where did you hear about this?"

"There's quite a lot about it in tonight's *Chronicle*. One of the chaps had it on the bus coming home. Hasn't ours come yet?"

"I think I heard someone put it through the letter-box five minutes ago." Anthea jumped up.

"They're giving away a thousand pounds or something," observed Roland, which served to hasten her footsteps.

He heard the rustle as she picked up the paper from the mat, and then she came back, much more slowly, into the room, staring at the front page of the *Cromerdale Chronicle* so fixedly that she nearly fell over a chair in her path.

"It's two thousand pounds," she said hoarsely. "The *Chronicle* are backing it too. And it says the competition's open to all types of singer, from vaudeville to operatic."

"Crumbs! There'll be a stampede!"

"No. It's limited to those who have made at least one professional appearance," explained Anthea, reading rapidly down the column. "Oh," – she looked up – "do you suppose a Masonic Dinner counts?"

"Since you were paid for it – yes," declared Roland confidently.

"It was only ten pounds," Anthea said humbly.

"That was all you were worth at the time," was the candid reply.

"Oh, Rollie," – she stopped and looked solemn – "it's as though it were meant to be. Like – Fate."

"It is, rather," agreed Roland, pleased to have been the forerunner of Fate, as it were.

"If only Miss Sharon will let me! She's dead against any competitions or engagements or anything like that in these early days. And it says here that the winner will be offered T.V. appearances."

She looked so anxious that Roland said:

"Cheer up. You haven't won it yet. Though I bet there's not another voice in this town to compare with yours. It's the chance of a lifetime, An! You must talk the Rose of Sharon round. Don't tell me that a few T.V. appearances are going to do you real harm. And once you've collected your two thousand and fulfilled your obligations, you can start in on the serious studying."

"Who's talking before I've won it now?" retorted Anthea. At which they both laughed. And, on this cheering sound, their mother returned.

The news about Mr. Benton was better than they had hoped. At least he had rallied well, though the doctor had been severe about his having gone back to work too soon, and emphatic that he must now stay out for a long time.

"But Mr. Prentiss was so kind!" Mrs. Benton exclaimed. "He told your father in front of me that his job would be waiting for him whenever he came back. And he said he would be on full pay for three months longer, and half-pay indefinitely after that. Considering all the sick-leave Dad's had already, I think it was handsome. But" – she paused and looked anxiously at her daughter – "I'm sorry, dear. This isn't going to be any help over what we were discussing."

13

"That's all right, Mother! Don't even think about that at the moment," Anthea replied earnestly. "Wait until Dad's well."

Then she saw that Roland was bursting with information about the competition, and she kicked him smartly under the table and just mouthed the word, "Surprise!"

And, with the most enormous effort, he contained himself.

It was hard for Anthea during the next few days to keep her hopes to herself. For, with the resilience of youth, she was now almost as elated and hopeful as she had once been depressed. Even the grudging quality of Miss Sharon's consent could not dash her.

"It isn't at all the kind of thing I would have wanted for you," Miss Sharon said. "But I do see that, with your father ill and money short –"

She took the newspaper announcement and studied it.

"Rather a mixed panel of judges, I notice," she observed disparagingly. "Many of them what I would call *Show* people" – she had a very special way of looking down her nose as she said this – "rather than serious musicians."

"They say they hope to have a famous conductor there," Anthea pointed out defensively.

"Probably someone who will send his regrets at the last minute, and well they know it," retorted Miss Sharon. "That's why they don't venture to give a name. However, just in case someone worthwhile turns up, we must see that you sing something worthy."

"Something reasonably popular, too," Anthea countered quickly. "It's a very *general* sort of contest, Miss Sharon."

"Handel perhaps – or Gluck," went on Miss Sharon, without taking much notice of the interruption. "Or Haydn's 'With Verdure Clad'."

14

There was a slight silence. Then Anthea said, diffidently,

"You don't think something a little more dramatic? – something operatic?"

"You mean a popular Puccini air, of course," replied Miss Sharon drily. "I have a great respect for Puccini, and despise those who do not know that *Bohème* is a masterpiece. But that is *not* the right thing for a young beginner to try to put before the public."

Anthea was tempted to say that, if she were going to win two thousand pounds in open competition, she had got to put something pretty snappy before the public. But one glance at Miss Sharon's face told her not to waste her breath. She agreed to "With Verdure Clad", and the necessary application form was completed and sent in.

Two days later Anthea received her entry card, with the somewhat depressing information that she was thirtieth on the list.

"They'll all be dead or stupefied with boredom by the time they get to me," she lamented to Roland. But he determinedly cheered her with the assertion that she would wake them up all right when it came to her turn.

On the appointed day – a wet and depressing Thursday – Anthea took herself off to the Town Hall, divided between giddy hopes and sickening despair.

The contest was not open to the public, she was rather relieved to find, though several of the sponsors evidently considered it their right and privilege to be present, and the contestants were allowed to sit and hear each other if they wished. Anthea counted them anxiously, twice over, and found they numbered exactly thirty, which did nothing to brighten her view of her own position on the list.

The hall – built in the heyday of Regency architecture –

was quite exceptionally beautiful, with wonderful acoustics. It had no fixed seats, and it had been easy to set up chairs and tables for the judges about halfway down the hall. The aspiring artists were seated down either side, and each competitor was called up to the platform in turn, by name and number.

Anthea sat there doggedly through the whole of the morning session, which disposed of at least half the number. At first she suffered agonies of nerves with each competitor. Partly on their behalf, but mostly because she had to view each one as a deadly rival.

But, after a while, she began to feel more at ease. She tried to be objective, even to judge leniently. But she knew, with rising hope and relief, that no one so far had anything like the vocal equipment that she had.

So then she turned her attention to the panel of judges. Among them she recognised the excellent choir-master from the nearby cathedral town (at least he would be able to judge the merits of her "With Verdure Clad"!), a well-known variety artist, and a couple of men whom she could not name but whose faces were vaguely familiar to her, probably from the television screen, she decided.

In addition there was a well-dressed, interesting-looking woman – not young, but with an attraction which had nothing to do with age – and she evidently took the whole thing very seriously. This was in marked contrast to the man on her left. Good-looking, in a forceful rather intimidating way, he seemed bored most of the time, but occasionally roused himself to a glance of sardonic and incredulous amusement when some of the least gifted contestants paraded their offerings before the panel.

Unlike the others, who all made copious notes, he wrote nothing on the sheet of paper in front of him, and Anthea strongly suspected that he had found no one worthy of even

16

a brief comment so far. She was not sure if this cheered or scared her.

At the lunch interval she allowed herself only a light snack, and when she was coming back she ran into Neil Prentiss, who greeted her with a warmth and friendliness which cheered her.

"You're looking very radiant and charming on this dismal day," he said, taking in her appearance in one comprehensive, approving glance. "How is your father?"

She reported on her father's slight improvement, and then he went on,

"Are you hoping to get in to hear the competition? If so, come with me. I'm hearing the afternoon session."

"I'm – I'm a competitor," she confessed. "I've been there all the morning, but I don't think I come on until the end."

"Then I'm glad I chose the afternoon session," he declared, so heartily that she really felt he must mean it. "Who did they get for the judges, in the end?"

Anthea told him about the choir-master and the variety artist, and the two whose faces were vaguely familiar.

"Those will be Chester Vane and Anthony Bookham, I expect."

"Yes, I remember now," she agreed. "I've seen them once or twice on television. Then there's a very distinguished-looking woman, who evidently knows a lot about it –"

"Enid Mountjoy. She was a very successful concert and oratorio singer in her time. Teaches now in London."

"She's very attractive still," Anthea said. "Then there's a rather horrid, bored-looking man with a supercilious air, who never makes a single note and looks as though he wonders why he's there."

Neil Prentiss laughed and shook his head.

"I don't know who that would be. One of the directors, perhaps, who's just there to dress the board."

"He doesn't look quite like that," Anthea said doubtfully. "Oh, look, there he goes," she added in a whisper, as a tall, arresting figure crossed the corridor just ahead of them.

"That? Why, my dear girl, that's Oscar Warrender," exclaimed her companion, sounding quite excited. "The famous conductor! They never really expected to get him. It was just a try-on. If he hadn't been conducting last night in Liverpool – well, I must say we're honoured." And he laughed in a pleased sort of way, rather like a schoolboy whose headmaster has deigned to notice that he has scored six runs, Anthea thought.

"Is *that* Oscar Warrender?" She was both elated and perturbed. For to be heard by the most celebrated conductor in the country was an exhilarating challenge. But the idea that that cold-eyed man carried more weight than anyone else on the panel was disturbing.

"Cheer up!" Neil Prentiss patted her arm encouragingly. "At least he *knows* about it all, and you'll get a worthwhile opinion."

Encouraged by this thought, Anthea returned to the hall, to find that the ranks had thinned considerably by now. And her immediate neighbour – a small, elfin-faced brunette with laughing eyes – whispered,

"Have you heard? They turned down the lot."

"All of us, do you mean? – without even hearing us?" gasped Anthea indignantly.

"No, no. All those that they heard this morning. I've got a cousin who's related to someone in the know, and I had lunch with him, and he says some of the panel wanted to take a few of the competitors seriously. But Warrender – that's the one with the fair hair and the good opinion of

18

himself – said they weren't even funny, and hadn't a scrap of what he called star quality between them. There was a bit of an argument, but he carried his point. I must say it makes the grade seem pretty stiff."

It did indeed, and stealing a half resentful glance at the man who seemed to have swayed the others so ruthlessly, Anthea thought she detected a faint degree of satisfaction in his handsome, rather arrogant face. Really, he was odious! even if he *was* famous and a genius and all that.

The harsh verdict on the morning competitors seemed to have shaken the confidence of the remainder badly. At any rate, the next few contenders were rather wild and ragged. And they too, at a slight gesture from the man who seemed pretty well to have taken over, were thanked perfunctorily and told not to wait.

Then, quite near the end of the afternoon, Anthea's neighbour was summoned. And, although there was a good deal of nervous tension about her, she went boldly to the platform and launched into a sort of musical sketch.

She had very little real voice, and what she had was husky and rather curious, but she was quite extraordinarily funny and actually made the panel laugh. Even Oscar Warrender accorded her a faint smile. And then, suddenly, the sketch ended abruptly on a note of pathos, and the lightning change of mood, from gaiety to melancholy, was so effective that Anthea actually felt her throat tighten.

The chairman of the panel called the girl over – the first time this had happened – and asked,

"Where did you get your material, Miss Pine?"

"I made it up," said the small dark girl calmly, at which there was a ripple of interest right along the row of judges.

"Remarkable," observed the chairman.

"Quite brilliant," declared the famous variety artist.

And then the choir-master, speaking from one end of the

row to Oscar Warrender, sitting at the other end, said almost apologetically,

"Not exactly our line, I know, but –"

"On the contrary, I find it very much my line," replied the famous conductor, in a cool, well-modulated voice which carried ruthlessly well. "Miss Pine has a touch of the star quality I referred to. We aren't likely to find anything more unusual this afternoon."

This was manifestly unfair, of course, to the half-dozen still waiting, and the chairman hastily murmured something, which obviously left Oscar Warrender unmoved. The small dark girl was asked to go back and wait, and the next number was called.

A shy young man, with a large, lugubrious, completely untrained bass voice, boomed his way through his offering, and Anthea noticed that the famous conductor had now shut his eyes and appeared to be completely detached from what was going on around him.

"I'll *make* him take notice," she thought furiously. "How dare he behave like this? It's enough to take the heart out of anyone. If the others are scared, I won't be!"

And the heat of her anger sustained her right through the rest of the waiting time until – at last, at last – "Miss Benton, Number Thirty," was called.

"The last, I think," said the chairman, stout-hearted to the end.

"Thank God," observed the conductor, insufferably and perfectly audibly.

Sustained though she was by her anger, Anthea would have lost a good deal of her courage at that moment if she had not received from Neil Prentiss a brilliant and encouraging smile, as she walked to the platform.

"I'll sing for him!" she thought, overwhelmed by a rush of almost passionate gratitude. "I'll sing for him because he likes me and wants me to succeed. I'll forget about that arrogant beast –"

But, as she walked on to the platform, as though by some inner compulsion, her glance sought the arrogant beast, sitting there, his chin cupped now in a rather beautiful hand, his gaze fixed upon her with monumental indifference. And somehow she forgot about Neil Prentiss, after all, and sang for Oscar Warrender, because she knew that of all the people there he was, as Neil had said, the one who really knew all about it.

Nothing in his expression changed. Only he glanced down once, and in the strong light she could even see that his lashes were unexpectedly long and cast a deep shadow on his cheeks. And, for the first time that day, he wrote something down on the paper in front of him.

It is not always easy for a singer to hear him or herself. But Miss Sharon had taught Anthea, from the very beginning, that she must try to do so. And now – possibly because in the tension of the moment she almost stood outside herself, as it were – Anthea was able to hear her own full, bright, beautiful soprano voice rising on a splendidly firm line.

She knew she was singing well. She knew that Miss Sharon herself could have found no fault with the phrasing. Perhaps her breath-control was not perfect to the end. But then she was nervous and excited, and she could not get over the fact that even Oscar Warrender had written something down at last.

In the very last phrase she went slightly under the note, she knew. But she thought they would not hold that too much against her. They would know – even that beast of a conductor would know, surely? – that it had been a great ordeal to wait until the very end of the afternoon.

With almost painful anxiety, her glance moved along the

21

row of judges. The choir-master was leaning forward, faintly flushed, and Enid Mountjoy had stopped consulting her previous notes and was smiling. Even the variety artist nodded in a gesture of measured approval, while the chairman said frankly, "That's a splendid voice!"

"Completely without temperament, though," said Oscar Warrender coolly. "Just good raw material. There's no question about the real artist today, in my view. Miss Pine, in her individual way, is the worthwhile contestant."

The chairman fidgeted. It was evidently against all his intention that the final discussion should take place in front of the competitors, and he added hastily,

"Thank you, Miss Benton. Will you wait, please?"

Then he firmly gathered up his papers and ushered the others into one of the adjoining committee rooms, while Anthea and the dark girl, and two others who had been asked to wait, lingered aimlessly in what had now become the vast reaches of the audition hall, trying not to meet each other's eyes, or to look either hopeful or as though they hated each other.

This was much the worst part of all, for the judges took unbearably long, it seemed. And Anthea knew – as well as if she had been in that smaller room across the passage – that Oscar Warrender, of all people, was arguing away her chances.

"Just good raw material" he had called her, as though she were some insensitive lump. And, even as he had said the words, she had felt the impact of her performance on the others insensibly lessen.

At last the secretary to the chairman – an efficient and self-effacing gentleman noticed by no one until that moment – came back into the hall, and they all four rose instinctively to their feet.

In a pleasant, congratulatory tone, he told the small dark

girl that the panel of judges would like to see her. And to Anthea and the other two, he said,

"Thank you very much. The panel were very happy to hear you, and though they couldn't award you the prize, they hope to hear you on some other occasion."

It was said as nicely as possible. It was the kindly sugaring of a bitter, bitter pill. But only pride kept the tears from Anthea's eyes and enabled her to say huskily, "Congratulations," as the small dark girl hurried off.

Out into the long deserted corridors once more, into the cold world of reality and crushing disappointment, after the wonderful days of hope and illusion. She tried to answer when one of the others – a cheerful young tenor – remarked, "Well, I suppose it was something to get into the last four."

But in her heart she thought, "It was nothing! Nothing unless one was *first* in the last four."

It was all the difference between a career and no career for her. Her great chance was gone. And in Anthea there was born at that moment, more strongly and more agonisingly than ever before, the absolute conviction that, given the smallest chance, she *could* have been a singer.

She was crying when she finally stepped out into the darkened street. But she was alone by now, so it did not matter. Only now did she realise how desperately she had built all her hopes on this one afternoon. Only now did she find the acceptance of failure so utterly, utterly insupportable.

And if Oscar Warrender had not intervened – he who was supposed to know so much about it! – she would have stood a good chance. She knew it. She felt so certain of the fact that it seemed to her that he had snatched away her rights from her.

She *ought* to have had that precious prize. It was not

conceit which made her sure of that. It was inescapable knowledge. The other girl was good – very good. She had charm and originality. And, incidentally, she seemed nice, so that one could not actually grudge her her good fortune. But she simply did not *begin* to have a voice, in the real sense of the word. And that conductor – the great operatic expert who was supposed to have such wonderful judgment – had insisted on her having the prize.

At the fresh realisation of the injustice, Anthea allowed one deep sob to escape her. And, as she did so, she turned the corner of the Town Hall and ran full tilt into someone coming from the other direction.

"Oh, my dear!" It was Neil Prentiss's kind voice which fell upon her ears with infinite comfort, and he actually put his arms round her and gave her a warm, sympathetic hug. "Is it such a terrible disappointment?"

"Y-yes." She was past even pretending it was not. She could only take the handkerchief which he kindly offered, and scrub her eyes with it. "It meant – so much," she whispered. "It would have been the money for my tr-training. And – I know it's awful to say so – but I *did* have the best voice. I know it."

"I thought so too," he agreed instantly. "I can't imagine why Warrender chose otherwise. They always say he's a capricious creature, of course. I suppose geniuses often are. But I should have thought there was no possibility of doubt." He broke off, and gently released her, perhaps because she gave a movement of impatience. And then he added doubtfully, "He really is considered to know more about voices and voice-development than anyone in Europe. They say –"

"I don't care what they say!" interrupted Anthea, quite loudly and rudely. "I think he's an arrogant, self-satisfied

24

beast. He was putting on an act the whole time! Pretending he was too good even to attend to what was going on. That man doesn't really care about art or music or artists or anything else. All he cares about is the great Oscar Warrender himself." And, stepping back a pace, the better to look up at Neil Prentiss and emphasise her point, she cannoned violently into someone who was just emerging from a side exit.

"Pardon me," said a cold voice, and a quite painfully strong hand took her by the arm and put her aside. And then, as she stood gazing after him in mingled fury and dismay, Oscar Warrender crossed the pavement, got into a waiting car, and was driven away.

"Oh —" said Anthea, in a small, deflated sort of voice. And then, as courage reasserted itself, she added defiantly, "I'm *glad*! He can't often have heard home-truths about himself."

"Not often," agreed Neil Prentiss amusedly. "He's a bit of a god in his own circle, I suppose. Most great conductors are."

And then, perhaps in tribute to Anthea's rebellious explosion, he insisted on driving her home, and when he left her he said:

"Don't despair, my dear. If it's true that they can't keep a good man down, it's even truer that they can't keep a lovely, gifted girl down either."

The words were not going to win her any prizes, or compensate for the lost two thousand pounds. But Anthea felt indescribably grateful for them, and the glow of them carried her through the sad necessity of telling Roland she had lost.

During the next few days, even Anthea's resilience failed

25

her. She resolutely put her dreams behind her and took herself along to the only employment agency in Cromerdale, with the determination to find herself *some* sort of employment.

The result was not encouraging, for she had little to offer except a reasonably good general education, excellent health and a pleasing appearance.

"You mean *no* typing and *no* shorthand?" said the young woman behind the enquiry desk, as though Anthea had come in without the decent minimum of clothes on.

"I'm afraid not," admitted Anthea, feeling not quite nice to know.

"Well, I'll put you down, of course." The young woman spoke as though it would really be a waste of time. "And let you know if – well, we'll see –"

The words died away into a non-committal murmur, and Anthea went out into the street again. As she did so, a voice hailed her from the other side of the street, and Miss Sharon – usually the most cautious and distrustful of pedestrians – plunged straight into the mainstream of Cromerdale's morning traffic.

Someone honked a horn and someone else swore, and a woman near Anthea said, "There! did you ever? Some of the old ones are the worst." And then Miss Sharon was standing safely beside Anthea, trembling slightly, but whether from her adventure or because of some inner emotion as yet unexplained, Anthea was not sure.

"Miss Sharon, whatever made you do such a thing?" Anthea took her affectionately by the arm.

"I don't know," was the somewhat shaky reply. "At least, yes, I do. I had to speak to you, and I was afraid of missing you. You weren't at home when I called."

"But what's happened?" Intrigued and puzzled, Anthea

26

stared at her teacher, who was evidently labouring under a high degree of excitement.

"Come home," said Miss Sharon. "Come home with me now, and I'll tell you. It may help me to believe it myself."

And after that she would not say a word, in spite of Anthea's wildly curious enquiries, until they arrived at the small house near the bridge where she lived.

"Come into the music room." Miss Sharon took off her hat and tossed it on to a peg in the hall, with an air of abandon that made Anthea open her eyes wide. But she followed her teacher into the room at the back of the house. The room where she had first been told that she had it in her to be a real singer. The room where she had striven so hard to make "With Verdure Clad" a performance that would sweep her to success in the competition.

"Sit down," said Miss Sharon, and Anthea sat down.

"Now read that." And, in the manner of one producing a whole family of rabbits from a hat, Miss Sharon handed Anthea a typewritten letter.

Mystified, Anthea took it and looked at the address – 14, Killigrew Mansions, London, W.1 – which conveyed nothing to her at all. Then she read on:

"Dear Madam, – I have been asked to get in touch with you as the teacher of Miss Anthea Benton, one of the competitors in the Cromerdale Television Contest last Thursday. Someone who heard her on that occasion was sufficiently impressed to want to further her training, and I have been asked to undertake what I might call the overall direction of this. I shall be obliged, therefore, if you will acquaint Miss Benton with the contents of this letter, and arrange for her to come to London next

Tuesday (the 20th) when I will audition her at the above address at 3 p.m., and decide what her future course of instruction should be.

Yours sincerely,
Oscar Warrender."

"I don't – believe it!" whispered Anthea, divided between horror and rapture. "I don't believe it!"

"I couldn't either," said Miss Sharon. "I cried when I first read the letter."

"Oh, Miss Sharon, did you?" This information was almost as shattering as the letter, for Anthea simply could not imagine her strict and self-contained teacher shedding tears.

"Of course," was the reply. "What else could I do? It's the sort of thing one dreams of – asks God on one's knees for – but never expects to have really happen. That you – that a pupil of mine – should be considered worthy to have her studies directed by Oscar Warrender!"

"*That's* not the best part of it!" declared Anthea disgustedly. "In fact, it's the only fly in the ointment. I can hardly bear the thought of being under the authority of that odious man, but –"

"He is a genius," stated Miss Sharon coldly. "And they're not so common, Anthea. Be thankful that he even knows that you exist."

"I don't think he wants to know it," muttered Anthea a trifle sulkily. "I can't imagine how he was persuaded to take this on. But someone – but *who*? – must have talked him over, or agreed to pay him handsomely or something. I can't imagine who would *care* enough – either about me personally or about my possibilities as a singer," she added honestly.

"I wondered," said Miss Sharon – rather naïvely,

Anthea thought – "if perhaps it were really he himself. That he secretly thought you very fine and decided to take you in hand, but wanted to remain anonymous."

"Oh, dear Miss Sharon!" Anthea laughed at this flight of fancy. "He wouldn't think of anything like that in a hundred years. No one could be less given to romantic impulses, I feel sure. And I just wish you could have seen the way he brushed me off, anyway. At least, no, I don't, for I'm still smarting at the humiliation of it. He practically said I was a lump –"

"A *lump*?" Miss Sharon was scandalised that even a genius should so far forget himself.

"Well, he said I was just good raw material," amended Anthea, "and that I had no temperament. And he took quite a lot of trouble – I could *see* he did – to influence the others against me. But it doesn't matter now. Someone thought differently. Someone" – she stopped suddenly and flushed and then went pale. "Oh," she said almost fearfully, "I think – perhaps – I know – who it is."

"Then keep the thought to yourself," said Miss Sharon, with heroic self-control and integrity. "Whoever is doing this for you has gone to some trouble to remain anonymous. The least you can do is respect his or her wishes."

"His," murmured Anthea softly. "His, I feel sure."

And, with a wave of gratitude that brought the tears to her eyes, she recalled what Neil Prentiss had said to her about its being impossible to "keep a lovely, gifted girl down".

CHAPTER II

IT was Neil Prentiss, of course. It had to be! And suddenly she wanted it to be Neil with an intensity she could not quite explain to herself.

Perhaps, after his previous generosity to the family, this was almost too much to accept. But he had understood so well about her crushing disappointment. He had felt the full injustice of it himself. And then he had told her so warmly how he genuinely admired her gifts and how, although he was no singer himself, he was passionately interested in singing as an art. It all added up to one thing only. It was to Neil Prentiss that she owed this glorious, this undreamed-of chance.

The only part of the arrangement which did surprise her was that he should have given Oscar Warrender authority over her. He knew – none better! – how she felt about the conductor, and he must know that she would be a good deal dismayed by the thought of actually working with him.

On the other hand, she had seen for herself that to Neil Prentiss that cold, authoritative man had a knowledge and judgment second to none. He must have felt – and rightly so, she had to admit – that this consideration must override any personal prejudice or antipathy.

For an hour or more Anthea and Miss Sharon continued to discuss the unbelievable event. And, as each aspect came under her dazzled attention, Anthea realised more and more that the short, unemotional, typewritten letter had altered her whole life.

"I hope he won't simply hear me and then say I'm not worthy of his attention," she said nervously.

But Miss Sharon pointed out that he had apparently already made some sort of agreement. Therefore for some probationary period at least, she would be given a chance to prove herself.

"And I will," thought Anthea. "I will. I'll make him eat his few contemptuous, condescending words about me one day!"

At home once more, she had to explain at some length before her mother could understand or believe what had happened. The more so that it was only then that she heard about the abortive attempt to win the television contest.

"You poor child, how did you keep it to yourself?" she cried. "Such a bitter disappointment."

"It doesn't matter now," Anthea said, smiling. And that was true. No disappointment, no slight, no injustice mattered now. Thanks to Neil Prentiss, she was to have a second golden chance.

Even to her mother she said nothing about her secret belief, and enjoyable speculation about her possible benefactor was the chief topic of conversation in the Benton household during the next few days.

Miss Sharon wrote to confirm the appointment, and she even generously declared herself willing to pay Anthea's fare to London. But this proved unnecessary, as by return of post there came a second-class return ticket (no silly unnecessary extravagances, Anthea was almost relieved to see) and a ten-pound note, to which there was attached a typed slip saying, "For meals, taxi-fares and sundries".

"He thinks of everything, the darling!" thought Anthea. And she was *not* referring to Oscar Warrender.

Tuesday was a beautiful, sunny, hopeful sort of day, and as she sat in the train Anthea thought that few people could have known such depths of despair and such heights of joyous excitement in the space of a couple of weeks.

It was two o'clock when she arrived at the big London terminus. But she had lunched on the train, and she took a taxi immediately to Killigrew Mansions. Then, having ascertained exactly where she had to go, she went into St. James's Park, where she sat in the sunshine, suddenly strangely short of breath, and tried to still the uneven beating of her heart, now that the test was so near.

She wished now, quite fervently, that the great conductor had *not* heard her candid opinion of him, in the rain, outside Cromerdale Town Hall. At the time, it had seemed a wonderful gesture of bravado. But now – alone in London, a very long way from home, and about to beard the great man in his own home – she felt it had been one of her less happy impulses.

The sound of Big Ben striking a quarter to three drifted across the Park and, gathering the remnants of her courage around her, Anthea walked back to Killigrew Mansions and took the lift to No. 14 which seemed to occupy, she noticed, most of the top floor. Here, a pleasant-faced woman – housekeeper rather than family, she thought – admitted her to a large and handsome apartment.

"Come through to the studio. Mr. Warrender won't keep you a minute," the woman said. And she took Anthea down two or three steps into a beautiful, lofty room, which had windows along one side, giving a splendid view across the Park to the Foreign Office.

There was no one in the room. But, as Anthea stood there, nervously taking off her gloves, the conductor came in by a side door. He greeted her quite courteously, and told her to take off her hat and sit down. Nothing in his expression indicated that he recalled the circumstances of their last meeting, but she could not really believe that he did not remember every detail of it.

"Tell me about your experience so far," he commanded. And when she gave him the length of time she had been studying, he made a disparaging little grimace and muttered, "Practically a beginner."

"I know it isn't very long," Anthea said defensively. "But Miss Sharon — my teacher — tells me that I have at least the advantage of an even scale and a — a natural placement."

"You don't say," he replied, with dangerous politeness, and she wished she had kept that bit to herself. "Well, come along and let's hear you."

He spoke as though he had never heard her before, and she actually wondered for a moment if he had forgotten!

But then, as he sat at the piano, taking her through subtly graded exercises and gradually extending scales, she was convinced again that he had forgotten nothing which had happened on that wet Thursday in Cromerdale.

Finally, he said, "I should like to hear you sing a song or an aria. What do you do in that line?"

She thought rebelliously of Miss Sharon saying that a Puccini aria was not the right thing for a young beginner to put before the public. But then he was not the public. He was the man who had said she was just raw material, with no temperament. And, a trifle defiantly, she said,

"I'll sing Mimi's aria from the first act of *Bohème*, if I may."

"You may." For some reason or other, he smiled at that, and she could not help seeing what an extraordinarily attractive smile it was. It did not actually warm those cold, uncomfortably penetrating grey eyes, but it lifted the corners of his arrogant mouth and softened it slightly.

He gave her the opening phrases of the recitative on the piano, and she began. She thought all the time of what he had said about no temperament, and she poured every ounce of feeling she had into her voice, giving the full power and purity of her really remarkable organ.

Halfway through he stopped her, made a pencil marking on the score and asked, "To whom are you singing this air?"

"Why, to – to you," she said, somewhat taken aback.

"No, no!" He sounded impatient. "You're on a stage. It's the first act. You made your entry just a few minutes ago. To whom are you singing?"

She was confused and a little frightened by his tone, which seemed to suggest that she was semi-idiotic.

"To – to the audience, I suppose."

"My God!" He passed both his hands over his smooth fair hair and observed to no one in particular, "And she thinks she's going to be an artist!"

Anthea bit her lip, and thrust back an unfamiliar desire to weep.

"To – to Rodolfo," she stammered. "To the tenor. I didn't quite understand what you meant."

"So I gather. Have you ever read this libretto right through?"

"Y-yes."

"Well, as you discovered at the third guess, you're singing this to Rodolfo. It's almost a conversation piece with a young man who has just begun to stir your romantic interest. You're a sick girl, innocently flirtatious, not asking very much of life, even a little unsure of yourself. Do you understand that?"

"Y-yes."

"Then why, in heaven's name, did you think it necessary to bellow your pretty confidences at the wretched young man in full voice?"

She didn't know. She only knew that she had wanted him to realise that she had some temperament, and a voice whose full beauty and power he had not perhaps suspected when he heard it before. She wished she could have explained. But she could only stand there, with her head bent and her lips trembling slightly.

"Try it again."

"G-give me a minute." She swallowed hard.

"What do you mean – give you a minute?" She was silent, and suddenly he looked up and said, with irritation, "Oh, for heaven's sake! If you're going to work with me, you must learn not to cry as easily as that. Tears bore me and make me nervous."

She could not really imagine that anything made him nervous. But she muttered, "I'm sorry."

Then he got up and came over to her and, to her inexpressible surprise, took both her hands in his.

"Stop being a little fool," he said, not unkindly. "Tears and singing don't go together. Come here beside me at the piano." And, still keeping one of her hands, he made her come back to the piano with him. He even continued to hold her hand in a firm, light clasp while he sketchily played through the air on the piano with the other hand. He spoke the words of the aria, as he did so, making her see exactly where subtle emphasis and darker or lighter shading of the tone could convey meaning and emotion without once overdoing the effect.

"She's a little gay, a little sad," he explained. "Nothing will ever be really solid or secure for her, and she knows it in her heart. But it's not great tragedy. Just tenderness and pathos. Now go back and try again. And look at me while you're singing."

She went back to stand in the curve of the grand piano, her eyes fixed upon him, her mind struggling to retain everything he had told her. And, for the first time in her life, Anthea seemed to empty herself of her own identity, so that something else slipped in and took its place – the identity of the girl he had described.

It was not possible to hold it all the time, and once she looked away from that clever, vivid face with the compelling grey eyes. But he said, quietly and authoritatively, "Look at me!" And she looked back and, in some inexplicable way, the spell was upon her again.

At the end, he did not tell her if she had done well or badly. He simply said, "How soon can you get yourself settled in London and start serious study?"

"You – you mean," stammered Anthea, "that you're going to take me?"

"Of course." He looked surprised. "You don't suppose I should waste this time on you if I didn't intend to train you, did you?" He spoke a little as though she were a performing dog, she noticed. "It was only a question of how far back we had to start."

"I can get settled in London just as soon as you say," she exclaimed eagerly, almost afraid that this wonderful, incredible chance might be snatched from her even now if she delayed in any way. "It's for you to say."

He seemed to think so too, for he did not accord this declaration of obedience even so much as a passing smile of indulgence. Instead, he began to make rapid suggestions and propositions. And, after no more than half an hour of arranging and telephoning, the thing was done, and Anthea received instructions to be in London on the following Monday, and to report once more at his flat at the same time in the afternoon.

And then, just as she was about to take her leave, he said, almost carelessly,

36

"You have a splendid lyric voice. I couldn't let them award you the prize in that absurd competition. You would have been ruined in a year or so. As it is, when I have finished with you" – he did smile then, with a faint touch of satisfaction which she found disturbing – "you may be worth something. Remember – here at the same time next Monday."

Both the words and the air implied instant dismissal. But Anthea was so astounded by what he had said that she found the courage to stand her ground and demand,

"What exactly do you mean by that? Did you talk the other members of the panel out of awarding me the prize because you thought me *too good*?"

"No. I didn't think you good at all," he replied, with crushing candour. "But I realised that you had a fine organ which, so far, you were not mistreating. For that, incidentally, your teacher may take full credit. And I was not prepared to be a party to having that voice ruined. That's all."

"But" – she could not hide her indignation – "that two thousand pounds would have helped pay for my training! That's what I wanted it for."

"Oh, no." He shook his head. "Once you found easy engagements coming your way, you would have been content to accept them and let any further work go. For a year or two you would have exploited your voice instead of developing it. You would have lived on your vocal capital, as hundreds – thousands – do today. And presently the organ you were abusing would have been damaged beyond repair, and you could no more make your vocal chords obey you than one can make a broken zip-fastener work again."

"But you couldn't *know* that I would have done that," she protested, still indignant. "You're just assuming that I'm a fool –"

"Of course," he agreed coldly. "There are so many more fools than wise people in the world, and I had no reason to think you among the minority."

She swallowed that as well as she could. But she was determined not to abandon the argument until she had settled one other point.

"You were not to know that some – some unknown benefactor was going to come forward and offer me the right training," she pointed out. "What if nothing had happened? What if I had been left with my voice safely intact, but with absolutely no chance of training and developing it?"

"You would have found a way if you have anything in you," he returned indifferently. "The artist who cannot conquer difficulties is not going to be much of a success. Remember that. For the way is not going to be easy, I promise you."

She remembered it. She remembered it all the way home. And particularly did she remember the faintly cruel tone of amusement in which he had uttered the warning. As though he rather enjoyed the idea of her having to struggle along a difficult road.

But that was not all she had to remember. As she journeyed back to Cromerdale on that unforgettable June day, she dazedly reviewed all that had happened to her.

Even now, she could not believe that everything had been arranged with relatively little fuss. But it seemed that when Oscar Warrender wished a thing done, it was as good as accomplished then and there.

Not for him the petty worrying about lodgings or timetables or expenses – or the relative merits of this and that. He said she was to take up residence in London. That was sufficient. Just a short telephone call and apparently a place was immediately found for her in a students' boarding-house in Kensington. And, even on that first afternoon, he had drawn up her scheme of studies with an exactness which made Anthea open her brown eyes wide.

For her actual singing lessons he decreed that she should go to Enid Mountjoy, which relieved and pleased her immensely, for she had been greatly impressed by the interesting, elderly, well-dressed woman on the board of judges, who so obviously knew what she was doing, and took such a conscientious interest in each competitor.

For languages – "Your Italian is pretty poor," he had said, "and I suppose your French and German are no better" – she was to go to a high-pressure language school. And for her overall musical training and operatic coaching she was to attend twice a week at the flat in Killigrew Mansions.

"Unless," he had added, "I am rehearsing or travelling, in which case we will make some other arrangement. But the most important thing for you to understand is that you will be expected to work as you have probably never worked before. I am not interested in amateurs, and to me laziness is the cardinal sin. Keep that well in mind in the coming months, and we may get on all right."

She had taken note of that disquieting "may". But she would have agreed if he had ordered her to walk all the way back home.

She liked him no better than she had in the beginning, and she was a good deal afraid of him. But she was already under his spell. That spell which one critic had once declared could make a third-rate performer second-rate, a second-rate one almost first-class, and a first-class artist scale heights never dreamed of before in his or her career.

Anthea wondered in which category she was listed in the

Warrender mind. Third-rate, she greatly feared, in spite of those faintly encouraging words when she was going. But terrifying though that audition had been, it had inspired her with an iron determination to prove that she *could* do all that he demanded of her. His criticism might be cruel and stinging, but the odd thing was that it made one avid for that word of almost unattainable praise which – surely, surely – he must occasionally dispense.

When at last she reached home, to find a wildly excited Roland and her mother waiting to hear every detail, she discovered that it was extraordinarily difficult to convey to them just what effect Oscar Warrender had had upon her.

It was comparatively easy to describe her hopes and fears as she had entered the flat in Killigrew Mansions. It was even simpler to list the questions asked and detail the arrangements made. But when she tried to re-create the scene of the audition, her mother was appalled to hear that she had actually been made to cry.

"Oh, it didn't really matter," Anthea assured her easily. "And somehow it – loosened the tension or something. Anyway, he was a bit sorry, I think" – she was not really at all sure about that – "and then he explained exactly what he meant. He's perfectly odious in many ways, of course. But he's a genius. I accept that now. He has a quality of inspiration which has nothing to do with either liking or disliking him. I've never known anyone in the least like him before."

Her mother looked doubtful and not a little troubled.

"I can't say that I feel very satisfied with the idea of your being almost completely under his jurisdiction," she said, frowning, while even Roland looked somewhat perturbed. "He doesn't sound at all a nice man to me."

"Oh, he's not!" Anthea laughed. "He's a beast, I tell
40

you. But" – suddenly she smiled and her eyes sparkled with a sort of inner fire – "he made me sing as I've never sung before. I felt I *was* Mimi for those incredible five minutes."

"Well, at any rate he seems to be a practical genius," Roland remarked. "You say he's got you fixed up with coaching and language classes and lodgings – the lot – so that you can begin next Monday? That is hustling, if you like. I'm surprised you told him you could be ready in time."

"Are you?" Anthea smiled again, as though she recalled something which puzzled her. "So am I now. But at the time it never occurred to me to do anything but agree to everything he suggested."

Crowded though her last weekend at home was, of course she made time to go and see Miss Sharon and give her a detailed account of all that had happened – including Oscar Warrender's grudging comment that her teacher must take credit for the fact that she was not mistreating her voice.

At this very meagre compliment Miss Sharon glowed with almost girlish ardour and was moved to prophesy rashly,

"You'll go far, Anthea. You'll go right to the top. With your gifts and his guidance you can't fail. You lucky, lucky girl!"

Anthea knew she was lucky – if not for quite the reasons Miss Sharon meant. And, on the way home, she suddenly came across the author of this almost unbelievable luck. Neil Prentiss came out of a house some yards ahead of her and, without seeing her, walked rapidly towards his car, parked farther down the street.

"Mr. Prentiss!" She broke into a run and, at the sound of her voice and her footsteps, he turned, and a smile of unmistakable pleasure and welcome brightened his good-looking face.

"Why, hello!" he said, and held out both his hands, so that it was perfectly natural to clasp both of them and stand smiling up at him, in slightly breathless eagerness.

"Mr. Prentiss, I'm so glad I saw you! I'm going to London on Monday and —"

"So it worked!" he exclaimed. And then looked so indescribably embarrassed and put out that she guessed he could have bitten his tongue out.

There was only one thing to do. To pretend for all she was worth that she had not heard his interruption nor guessed his secret.

"I specially wanted to tell you," she explained, "because you were so wonderfully good over Dad, and so kind and understanding about my disappointment at the T.V. contest. Something almost incredible happened! Someone — I can't imagine who, but I suppose it might have been one of the panel — apparently decided I was worth training, and I was summoned to London and auditioned by Oscar Warrender, of all people. And he's taking on the overall direction of my training and —"

She stopped for lack of breath and laughed and found that she was still holding both Neil Prentiss's hands.

"Isn't it *wonderful*?" she cried, as the full realisation of it all swept over her again.

"Wonderful," he agreed, looking at her as though it were the radiance of her joy and enthusiasm which he found wonderful. "But I'm not entirely surprised. *Someone* had to recognise the beauty of that voice and do something about it. How does Oscar Warrender rate now?" And he laughed mischievously down at her.

"I can't like him. I never should," she declared. "But I suppose that isn't necessary. The fact is that he's the most

42

extraordinary, inspiring creature, and even while you could slap him across that handsome, arrogant face, you want madly to do exactly what he tells you. Does that sound crazy?"

"Absolutely," he assured her amusedly. "But it has the ring of truth. Even the great Peroni is reported to have said, 'I could kill him – except that I should be half the artist without him, and the most heartbroken mourner at his funeral.'"

"*She* said that?" Anthea was impressed. "So great a singer, and she still feels his power and acknowledges his authority. I begin to think Miss Sharon is right, and that I'm incredibly lucky to have him even notice my existence."

"Believe me, you couldn't be in better hands," Neil Prentiss assured her earnestly, and she rather thought this was his way of justifying his hard choice.

"I'm sure you are right," she said gently. "And to the day I die I shall be grateful to whoever gave me this wonderful chance."

"You dear, appreciative girl! I wish you all the luck in the world in London," he declared. And, to her astonishment, he bent and lightly kissed her flushed cheek. "Bless you. I'll hope to see you sometimes when I come."

"Oh, indeed you shall!" she cried in delight. "Do you sometimes come to London?"

"Every few weeks," he assured her. And then he took his leave, and she walked on alone through the late summer evening, warm to her very heart at the thought that Neil Prentiss would still have some place in her life.

The visit to Miss Sharon had been Anthea's last port of call, and as she made her way homeward now, she silently took leave of one familiar landmark after another. She would be coming back, of course – often. But the conviction was growing upon her that the Anthea who returned to

43

Cromerdale would never be quite the same person again.

The days of her sheltered, largely untroubled, uninhibited girlhood were slipping away. When she came back next time she would already have had some experience of the world, acquired some knowledge of the professional way which lay before her. Above all, in some subtle, inexplicable way, she knew that the seal of Oscar Warrender would have been set upon her, for good or ill.

The next morning the final goodbyes were said – briefly to Roland, as he was rushing off to school – and more lingeringly and with some emotion to her mother. Her goodbyes to her father had been said in hospital the previous day, and she still recalled with happiness the light of pride and interest in his eyes as he had listened to her plans.

"I wish I didn't have to leave you at such an anxious time," she said, as she hugged her mother goodbye. "But I think Dad's out of the wood now. And of course I *am* only four or five hours' journey away. I could rush back at a moment's notice if – if you felt there were any special need."

"Don't worry. I'm not summoning you back from the really important work of your life," her mother promised. "I have an idea your Oscar Warrender would think poorly of family claims versus professional ones."

"His isn't absolutely the last word," Anthea declared, with a toss of her head. And on this final declaration of defiance, she departed from Cromerdale on the great London adventure.

When she said those words, she had meant them. But when she recalled them, as she stepped into the elegant silence of Fourteen Killigrew Mansions that afternoon, she found them peculiarly empty and pointless. For, of course, she had chosen the exact expression which summed up Oscar Warrender's place in her life from now onwards. His *was* the last word. In everything.

44

A little to her relief, he was not alone this time. Enid Mountjoy was also there, and she greeted Anthea kindly though a trifle formally.

"I am glad we are going to work together," she said. "I thought your voice very beautiful when I first heard it. In some circumstances I think I should have had to insist on awarding you the prize. But" – she shrugged expressively – "there were other considerations."

"I understand," Anthea told her quietly, and she simply could not help glancing at Oscar Warrender.

She was not surprised to find him smiling faintly in that cold, arrogant way of his. Very pleased he looked at having done her out of two thousand pounds because he judged her too much of a fool to be trusted to spend it wisely!

For quite a while Enid Mountjoy talked to Anthea about her development so far and her projected studies. She went to the piano once, to illustrate some point she wanted to make, and as she walked across the room, Anthea saw that she was slightly lame. But she moved with exceptional grace all the same.

During this conversation Oscar Warrender allowed her to take charge entirely, and contented himself with merely interjecting a trenchant comment from time to time – often of an uncomplimentary, nature.

"You must not expect miracles at this early stage, Mr. Warrender," Enid Mountjoy told him with a smile.

But he brushed that aside.

"Mediocrity is easy to attain," he said contemptuously. "The miraculous is the least one must aim at. I've told her that she has a hard road in front of her. Don't give her any comfortable illusions."

"If I did you would have no difficulty in dispelling them, I'm sure," was the amused retort.

"Well, she has an essentially amateurish approach at the

45

moment," he said, speaking of Anthea as though she were either stone deaf or not present. "That's the first thing to put right."

"We'll do our best," replied Enid Mountjoy, with an encouraging smile at Anthea. Then she got up and said, "I must go now. Shall I drop you off at your boarding-house? It's on my way and I have my car here. Is your luggage downstairs?"

"Yes." Anthea got up, too eager to take this opportunity of furthering their acquaintance. "If you would be so kind —"

"You're not free," cut in the conductor drily. "This was only the preliminary discussion. You have a lesson, even if you have forgotten it."

"On the very first day! — on her way from the station?" Even Enid Mountjoy seemed surprised.

"On her very first day — on her way from the station," Oscar Warrender confirmed coolly. "If she is going to fill in some of the lamentable gaps in her knowledge, she can't start too soon."

"Very well." Enid Mountjoy bowed gracefully to inexorable circumstances and then, turning to Anthea, she said, "I'll see you tomorrow at ten. I'm within walking distance of your boarding-house, and any of the students will tell you the way."

Then she went away, and Anthea felt a little as though she were being abandoned.

"Now we'll get down to work," the conductor decreed. "Last week we just played at it."

That was not at all the way Anthea would have described that harrowing scene over the Mimi aria. But she soon began to see what he meant.

At least, she saw what he meant about the real work beginning now. What he meant by his crisp, curt words of

46

explanation and direction she found much more difficult to follow, particularly at one point when she found herself badly trapped over a particularly difficult entry.

In the end, he asked, with an air of dangerously diminishing patience, "I take it you do know how to read music?"

"Y-yes, of course," she stammered.

"Well, read it, then!" he shouted, crashing his hands down on the piano keys with a force that made her nearly jump out of her skin. "If you can't pay attention to the simplest instructions –"

"They aren't simple instructions," she suddenly heard herself shout back at him. "You're not very good at explaining, if you must know. You assume I know all sorts of things I can't possibly know, and you don't bother to make yourself clear."

A deathly silence succeeded this incredible outburst, during which she prayed for the ground to open and swallow her up. Then he said, almost pleasantly, "You mean *I'm* the one who is lacking in intelligence?"

"N-not that – no. But you – you –"

"Do go on," he said gently. "I'm devoured with curiosity." And he leaned forward to pencil something on the music in front of him.

Suddenly she knew that this was a trick of his when he wanted to shake someone's nerve. And, to her stupefaction, she found herself saying,

"Do you really want to know what I have to say? Because, if so, it would be more polite to look at me."

"I am not a polite man," he returned coolly. But he sat back then and regarded her, with eyes so cold that they were like shadows on an ice-field, she thought. They even had that same strange tinge of blue in them.

"I – I didn't mean to be rude to you" – Anthea swal-

47

lowed nervously — "but you scared me and —"

"For someone scared you're doing very well," he interrupted drily. "This is the first time I've been taken to task about my method of approach. But go on."

"I — I just want to say that nearly everything you're telling me is new to me. I can't take it all in at once. It's useless if I don't understand from the beginning. If you'd be just a little more patient —"

"Shall we try again?" he said quietly, and she was not at all sure if the query contained reassurance or menace.

They tried again, and by some miracle of good fortune she contrived to do exactly what he wanted. She got no praise for it. He merely said, "Why couldn't you have done that before?" But at least that brought her safely to the end of her lesson.

Then, just as she was putting on her things, he enquired abruptly,

"Have you ever been to an opera?"

"Oh, yes. Three times," she told him. "But only when a touring company came to the nearest big town, of course."

"What did you hear?" he enquired curiously.

"*Tannhauser, Fledermaus* and *Wozzeck.*"

He laughed at that. He laughed so much that she could hardly believe her ears. And she thought she had never seen anything so handsome as that vivid, almost dangerously intelligent face when the eyes were sparkling and his lips were drawn back from his teeth in that almost devilish expression.

She had to smile, puzzled though she was. And finally she asked, "Is that so very funny?"

"Indescribably so," he assured her, suddenly in excellent humour. "It's the funniest mixture I've ever heard, and a wonderful comment on the material provided for the operatic beginner. What did you make of *Wozzeck*?"

"Very little," she said frankly.

"So I should imagine. Then you've never heard a Verdi opera on a stage?"

She shook her head.

"How wonderful," he said softly, almost to himself, and she could hardly credit the depth of feeling which suddenly warmed that usually cold, incisive voice. "How wonderful to be hearing a Verdi opera for the very first time." Then he turned to her, and said in something more like his usual tone, "You had better come with me tonight. They're doing *Otello* at Covent Garden."

"Come with you? To the *opera*, do you mean?" She could hardly believe her ears – this time for the words rather than the tone.

"Yes, of course. Do you think you can get there on your own, or shall I fetch you?"

"Oh, no! I expect I can manage all right." She was trembling with excitement. "In fact, of course I can," she added hastily, not wanting to seem in any way helpless or unsophisticated.

"Then meet me in the foyer at ten past seven."

"Are you conducting?" she asked eagerly.

"No, of course not," he returned impatiently. "What do you suppose I should be doing in the foyer at ten past seven if I were conducting? Laurent is conducting. He's not as good as I am, but he's good." He stated that as a fact, without conceit or false modesty. "Ten past seven. And don't be late."

"Oh, I won't be!" Her eyes were sparkling and her colour high. "What do I wear?"

"Wear? Who cares what you wear?" he demanded comtemptuously.

"No – I mean is it evening dress? Because I haven't got a real one, and I thought perhaps –"

"Wear what you like," he told her indifferently. "No one is going to look at you."

And, on this deflating piece of information, he dismissed her from his presence.

CHAPTER III

DOWNSTAIRS once more, and still in a daze, Anthea let the hall porter summon a taxi for her. Not that she expected to indulge in many extravagances of this sort, now that she was entering on her student days. But she still had her luggage with her, as she had come straight to Killigrew Mansions from the train. And, in any case, she had no idea where her boarding-house might be, except that it was in Kensington.

As she drove along, she caught fascinating glimpses of places that seemed vaguely familiar from photographs she had seen in newspapers from time to time. But more than half her mind was still concerned with the scene which had just taken place.

Again there had been that extraordinary mixture of near-terror and almost breathtaking stimulation, and even now she felt both shocked and pleased to realise that she had actually stood up to the intimidating Oscar Warrender and answered him back.

She was not at all sure that he had thought any the less of her for that either. At least it had not prevented him from giving the incredible invitation to accompany him to Covent Garden that evening.

Quite a short drive brought her to the tall, rather shabby terrace house which was to be her home in future. And here she was welcomed very cordially by Mrs. McManus, the owner of the place. Mrs. McManus was a large, slightly flamboyant lady in her late sixties, with a fine speaking voice, admirable teeth and hair of somewhat bogus blackness.

Anthea guessed that she had once been a singer of sorts herself. And indeed, even as she conducted Anthea upstairs to her room on the first floor, she informed her that this was the case, and explained that her special partiality for boarding music students arose from her earlier experience in the operatic world.

"I never got further than a Rhinemaiden at Covent Garden," she confided to Anthea, "but on tour I had a big repertoire. Those were the days! Six weeks we'd do in Manchester and Liverpool, and four in Glasgow and Birmingham. And then there were dozens of places where we'd have a one-week stand. And crowded houses all the way. All they want now is pop nonsense or the goggle-box. Faugh!"

Anthea had never before met anyone who actually said, "Faugh!" And was – like most of us – quite intrigued to find how it was really pronounced by those who use it. But she expressed genuine interest in Mrs. McManus's past career, which evoked the kind assurance,

"I'll look after you, dear. Miss Mountjoy said you're from the Provinces and might need a bit of guidance, but you'll soon get to know the ropes. There are eight other music students in the house. Two strings, two wind and four vocals. So you'll feel quite at home."

Anthea said she was sure she would, and added – with sincerity – that she very much liked her room.

"Well, it's homely, and the food's good, though I say it myself," Mrs. McManus declared. "Goodness knows, I've been in too many theatrical lodgings in my life not to know what makes for comfort. To come home from a hard evening's work and try to sleep on a mattress that feels like potatoes — that's my ideal of hell," she added cheerfully.

Then, as Anthea looked round and smiled contentedly, she said, "Well, you get yourself unpacked and settled in, dear, and come downstairs when you hear the gong go. It'll be at five-thirty today. It's high tea instead of dinner because four of them are going to the opera tonight. It's *Otello.*"

"I know. I'm going too," explained Anthea, feeling delightfully in the swim of things already.

"Going to Covent Garden?" Mrs. McManus looked surprised. "But have you got a ticket? It's not much good going up on chance this evening, you know *Otello*'s a very popular opera these days, though once it was considered rather a connoisseur's piece," she added knowledgeably.

"Yes, I've got a ticket," Anthea said rather shyly. "At least, a — a friend is taking me."

Suddenly it seemed preposterous and boastful to say that Oscar Warrender was taking her.

"Well, you're a lucky girl," said Mrs. McManus heartily. "There was a terrific demand at the booking. But that was when they thought Warrender was conduct ng. Now he's not taking over until later in the season. But the other man's good too."

"So I've been told," murmured Anthea rather demurely.

"Not a bad start for your first night in London, I must say! To be taken to *Otello* at Covent Garden."

"That's what I thought," agreed Anthea happily. "There's just one snag. I — I think he's got quite good seats. Does it matter that I haven't a proper evening dress?"

"Not unless you're going to be in a box, and even then you can make do, except on a first night," Mrs. McManus informed her with authority. "Well, I'll leave you now to settle in." And with a brisk but friendly nod to Anthea, she went off downstairs.

Left alone, Anthea unpacked rapidly, and shook out the folds from her one party dress with particular care. She inspected it anxiously and tried to decide how it would measure up to other creations in the stalls or boxes of Covent Garden.

It was simply cut and a very pretty shade of apricot, which imparted a warm glow to her really beautiful skin. It was true that no one would mistake it for a Paris model. On the other hand, when she had put it on and surveyed herself in the mirror of her small wardrobe, she decided that it was somehow "her" dress, and that at least she would not disgrace her distinguished escort on this wonderful evening.

During the short time she had left, she wrote a hasty note to her mother, declaring -- with some over-simplification of the case -- that everything seemed to be working out wonderfully. And then, when a loud gong boomed, on the stroke of five-thirty, she went downstairs feeling both shy and excited.

As she entered the slightly shabby dining-room, it seemed to her that the place was full of people, all talking at once. And, unused as she was to this kind of thing, she hung back, a little undecided.

Mrs. McManus, however, spied her immediately and, bringing her forward, rather in the manner of a capable nanny who had no intention of having her charge overlooked at the party, she made rapid and comprehensive introductions.

Anthea then discovered that the "two strings" were violin students, answering to the names of Bob and Toots (Toots being a charming red-haired girl with a slight but attractive cast in her left eye). The "two wind" were both young men, one studying to be a flautist and the other a horn-player. They talked almost incessantly to each other, and flung only an occasional word into the general conversation.

The "four vocals" consisted of an Irish tenor, unoriginally addressed as Paddy by everyone, a graceful, rather aloof girl called Sarah Albany, who sounded like a mezzo from her speaking voice, a gay little brunette, introduced as Toni Crann, and an equally gay blonde who said immediately to Anthea,

"Come and sit beside me and tell me all about yourself. My name's Vicki Donnington, and I'm not really regarded as a professional student. I just LIKE singing. It sounds dreadfully unambitious, I know, with everyone else scrambling to get to the top of the operatic tree. But I guess that's just the way I'm made."

Anthea smiled at her and said, "I think I rather like the way you're made."

The other girl laughed at that and observed shrewdly, "Well, at least it saves me from agonies of professional jealousy. Ma McManus says you're going to the Garden tonight, but in the front of the house. We're all in the amphitheatre, of course. How come you got a seat in the front, you lucky thing?"

"I'm – being taken," Anthea admitted.

"Then she's got a rich boy-friend," Vicki informed the rest of them with satisfaction. "How useful! Or someone who can pull a string – which might be even more useful, if it's the right kind of string. What's his name?"

Anthea took a deep breath and then, realising that prevarication would only land her in deeper waters, she elected for the simple truth and said,

"He's not a boy-friend *at all*. I – I just happen to be a pupil of Oscar Warrender, and he's taking me."

55

On the instant all conversation ceased and everyone stared at her incredulously. Then the horn-player said,

"You're going to the opera with *Oscar Warrender*? What on earth does it feel like?"

"Champagne and bitter aloes," replied Anthea who, until that moment, had had no idea that she possessed something of a gift for repartee.

The others shrieked in chorus, and Vicki Donnington actually patted her on the back and exclaimed,

"Oh, we're going to like *you*. What can we contribute to the occasion? Can I lend you anything? An evening bag or a stole – I've got a lovely golden one – or even your fare? I mean – we must make it a co-operative effort and see that you do us all proud. Oscar Warrender! Do you mind if I touch you?" And she gave Anthea a small, mischievous pinch.

Anthea laughed.

"It's terribly nice of you all to be so interested, and helpful. Of course I'm wildly excited. You see, it's the first time I've ever been to Covent Garden, for one thing –"

"The first time," echoed Vicki, "and she's going with Oscar Warrender. Oh, *do* borrow my stole! I'd love to think it had sat beside the great man, even if I hadn't. And it would go beautifully with your pretty dress, as a matter of fact."

Before Anthea could reply to that, however, Violet Albany asked curiously, "Do you know him well?"

"Yes. Tell us what he's really like," begged the gay little brunette. "We all know he's madly attractive, of course. One can see that much, even from the amphi. But they say he's a devil too. Is he?"

Anthea opened her lips to say just exactly what she thought of Oscar Warrender and the arrogant way he walked through life. But then something instinctive warned

56

her that this was the moment when she must start, exercising the discretion she would have to maintain rigidly during the coming months.

It was natural for them to want to hear personal details about one of the celebrities of their particular world. But, while maintaining a friendly and open manner, she would have to guard against being a source of casual gossip.

So with an air of good-humoured candour, Anthea contented herself with saying,

"I don't really know him personally. The – the friend who is paying for my training decided that he was the man to have the overall direction of it, and so I was sent along to be auditioned by him. He accepted me, I'm glad to say. But as for knowing him – I've met him only twice. Well, perhaps three times," she amended, suddenly remembering that unintentional encounter in the rain outside Cromerdale Town Hall.

"I say, you do have the right sort of friends, don't you?" observed Vicki admiringly. "I wish *I* knew someone who thought it a good idea to send me to Oscar Warrender."

"It wouldn't be any good if you had," declared the horn-player unkindly. "You'd be rejected out of hand. Warrender doesn't take merely talented people who want to sing. I didn't know he took *anyone*, to tell the truth. You must be exceptionally good." And he regarded Anthea with interest.

"Are you exceptionally good?" enquired Vicki frankly.

"I don't know. He doesn't give me that impression," Anthea admitted with a smile. "But I suppose these are early days for him to form a definite opinion."

"They say," said Sarah Albany sombrely, "that he can hear a voice in the raw and tell exactly what it *ought* to sound like when it's been properly trained and developed. And they also say that, once he gets a singer under his

57

hand, he knows just what he's going to do with that artist for the next five years."

"Do they?" Anthea felt slightly uncomfortable at the idea of anyone – particularly Oscar Warrender – knowing so much about her as that.

But then someone said it was time they were going, and immediately there was a great scramble to get ready.

"Are you going grandly in a taxi?" Vicki wanted to know. "Or would you prefer to come with us on the Tube?"

"Oh, I'll come with you, *please*," Anthea assured her.

"And wear my stole?" pleaded Vicki.

"If you really are so kind, and mean –"

"It's yours. Say no more," Vicki ordered her, and she raced away upstairs, to return in a matter of minutes, with a very lovely golden tissue stole draped over her arm.

"It's almost *too* beautiful," protested Anthea.

But Vicki would hear no argument. And certainly when it was put round Anthea it did wonderful things to the simple apricot-coloured dress, and made her feel that she could hold her own even in the company of Oscar Warrender.

On the way up to town, she alternated between rapturous excitement and nervous apprehension. To be going to Covent Garden at all was an event in the life of an inconspicuous Cromerdale student. But to be going in these special circumstances was to step out of obscurity into the highlight of drama.

For the moment it was wonderful to be just one in a company of gay contemporaries who shared the same interests as herself. It was – she admitted it frankly – very gratifying to be envied and questioned because she had the distinction of knowing Oscar Warrender.

But very soon this easy, lighthearted phase of the evening

would be over. She would be leaving the support of her pleasant new friends and be flung upon a social world entirely beyond her experience. There would be no one to smooth an unfamiliar path but the critical and intimidating conductor. And, whatever Oscar Warrender's gifts might be, he was certainly no path-smoother. Of that Anthea was quite sure.

As they streamed out of Covent Garden Tube station, along with dozens of other chattering enthusiasts, Vicki caught Anthea by the arm and said,

'Look, that building going on is the new – and much-needed – extension to the Opera House. Despite the glamour of the auditorium – and it's one of the loveliest opera houses in the world – backstage it's unbelievably primitive and crowded, and they desperately need new dressing rooms and rehearsal space. As you probably know, all the area around the Opera House used to be the fruit and vegetable market. When it moved out a few years ago it gave the Opera House the chance to expand – and in fact a whole new, exciting area is growing up now where the market used to be.'

Then, as they hurried along the side of the Opera House, she said,

"That's the stage door, where we wait sometimes for *hours* after a performance to see the stars come out. And that's the side entrance where we go in. Now I'll take you round to the front of the house and show you where you go. Don't look so solemn. You're going to *enjoy* yourself. Why, half the people here would willingly give their back teeth to change places with you tonight!"

And, when she had shown Anthea the beautiful porticoed entrance to the Opera House, she gave her arm a reassuring squeeze and exclaimed, "Have a wonderful time," before she slipped off to join her friends for an evening of much less inhibited enjoyment in the amphitheatre.

The lights and the crowds in the foyer bewildered Anthea at first, and she was seized with panic lest she should be unable to find the conductor among all these people. But then she saw him – indescribably distinguished in evening clothes, talking to a small, animated man with grey hair.

She approached somewhat diffidently and stood almost at his elbow for a moment or two before he realised she was there. Then he said, "Oh, hello. You found your way all right, then?"

"Yes, thank you. I came with some of the other students at my boarding-house. They were also coming and brought me by Tube."

He introduced his companion then, as "Max Egon, the producer," and added to the short grey-haired man, "This is the girl I was telling you about."

Immediately, of course, she was consumed with curiosity to know in what terms he had "told about" her. But the other man replied rapidly in German, which Anthea could not follow.

She did, however, know enough to gather that the conductor replied impatiently in the same language, "One day, one day. Too early to say yet." And then a bell rang, and Oscar Warrender said, "Come," and, taking her lightly by the arm, he ushered her towards the grand staircase, with its glittering mirrors and chandelier.

Until the moment he touched her, Anthea had always assessed his impact and attraction simply by his looks and the way he spoke. But as she felt those long, strong fingers close round her arm, with only the thin silk of Vicki's gold stole in between, she was immediately aware of a current of feeling that was electric in its primitive suddenness and violence. She felt the colour shocked into her face and then away again.

There was nothing even remotely familiar in his touch, and the complete indifference of his expression showed that the contact meant nothing to him. But for Anthea it was the most extraordinary and disturbing discovery she had ever made: that by the mere sense of touch this man could make her feel as though something had lit a fire within her.

As they passed up the great staircase and into the Grand Tier, more than one person turned to look at them. It was, of course, the first time in her life that Anthea had experienced the heady sensation of walking with the famous, and she felt almost light-headed with the strange, intoxicating novelty of it all.

She was not quite sure how much of her feeling was due to his touch on her arm, how much to the dazzling surroundings, and how much to the extraordinary experience of being a focus of interest. But, when she finally entered Oscar Warrender's box with him, and the full beauty of one of the loveliest opera houses in Europe burst upon her, she whispered half to herself and half to him,

"I can't believe it. I simply can't believe it!"

"What can't you believe?" he wanted to know.

"Everything," she exclaimed comprehensively. "It's like a dream – and then one wakes up. Like something one invents, but never really expects to come true. Th-thank you most awfully for bringing me."

"It hasn't begun yet," he replied, rather disagreeably. "If this side of the curtain dazzles you so completely, what's going to happen to you when you get to the other side?"

"The – other side?" she stared in fascination at the great velvet curtain, with its regal monogram. "The other side?" Then she turned to him impulsively, and this time it was she who put her hand on his arm. "Tell me truthfully – do you honestly think that one day I shall get to – the other side?"

61

"I don't know," he replied composedly, removing his arm from under her hand. "Only time will tell. But I shouldn't be wasting all this time and energy on you if I didn't feel there was some faint possibility that I could make something of you."

"You say 'make' as though you almost literally mean to — to mould me into something you want," she said a little apprehensively.

"Of course," he told her coolly. "That's exactly what I mean to do. I don't think you'll break in the process, because you're basically tough. But if you do," — he shrugged — "well, then I guessed wrong and you're — you're —"

He seemed to seek for a word, and she drily supplied it. "Expendable?"

"Precisely," he agreed, apparently slightly amused that she had got his meaning so accurately. And then the conductor entered the orchestra pit to the sound of applause, the lights were dimmed and, with great crashing chords, they were precipitated into the opening storm of *Otello*.

"*Expendable!*" thought Anthea, in angry disgust. "What a word for him to accept."

And then she thought no more about herself and Oscar Warrender, for she was sucked into the vortex of the drama on the stage, and for a while she was oblivious of anything but the terror and pity of it all.

She was unaware that the man beside her watched her a good deal in the faint light from the stage. Only when the curtain fell for the first interval, he said quietly,

"Yes, I think perhaps Egon was right."

"What?" she said vaguely, and turned her almost dazed glance upon him.

"You didn't understand what Max Egon said about you?"

She shook her head, still hardly interested in anything

but the shattering artistic experience of the last hour.

"He said, 'If she has the voice to match her looks and manner, she is a Desdemona.'"

"She –? He meant *me*?" Suddenly she was awake to what he was saying. "He meant that – that *I* might one day sing in this wonderful, wonderful opera?"

"No, he didn't mean anything of the sort," was the deflating reply. "He merely meant that you looked the part. So do lots of unsophisticated blondes. Few, however, ever learn to sing it."

"But you said just now –" she searched her mind for his exact words – "you said you thought perhaps he was right. What did you mean by that?"

"I meant that you reacted with some intelligence and seemed to having some feeling for the part," he replied drily. "At last I noticed you cried in the right places," and he smiled grimly. "Would you like to come out during the interval and have a drink or a coffee?"

"No, thank you." She shook her head, suddenly shy and overwhelmed. "I'll just sit here and – and think about it all."

He left her then, and she sat there alone, almost exhausted by the depth and the complexity of the emotions she had experienced that day. It seemed weeks since she had left home that morning. Cromerdale and her family circle were a whole world away from all this, and suddenly she felt inexpressibly lonely as well as excited.

If she could have rushed back to her mother after the performance, to tell her all about it – if she could have felt that somewhere outside this vast and glittering theatre she might run across Neil Prentiss – it would have been different. Perhaps in a few weeks' or months' time, when she was more at home in this strange setting, it would be better. But, sitting there now, in the splendour of Oscar Warrender's box, she had never felt more alone in her life.

She stared out across the opera house, at the people now beginning to filter back into the auditorium, and she knew none of them. Not one single person. It was the most extraordinary and disquieting experience for someone brought up in a place where one could scarcely go down the street to buy a packet of soap flakes without running into *someone* one knew.

The only person she knew in this vast throng was the man now coming back into the box behind her —

And then suddenly she remembered! and with a joy and relief beyond all expression, she leaned forward in the box and looked up into the far reaches of the amphitheatre.

Immediately a handkerchief and two programmes waved, and with warmth in her heart, she waved back.

"Who are the friends?" enquired her companion, in not very pleased surprise, she thought.

"It's Vicki and Sarah and Paddy and Toni," she explained expansively. "They're up there. Oh, it's wonderful to *know* someone here."

"You know me," he pointed out. But when she said naïvely, "That's different," he did not dispute the fact.

And then she looked at him and a sudden impulse came to her.

"Mr. Warrender," she said eagerly, "would you do something very, very kind?"

"I don't expect so. I'm not a very, very kind person," he replied, mimicking her tone with cruel accuracy. "But what do you want me to do?"

"Would you *please* look up at the amphi and smile at where those programmes are waving. It — it would mean a lot to them."

"Oh, I don't think —"

"They've been very kind to me," she pleaded quickly.

"Vicki even lent me this stole so that I shouldn't feel a bit drab in your company."

"You don't say!" He glanced at the stole. "It's charming," he conceded unexpectedly.

Then he leaned forward, looked up at the amphitheatre and smiled at the fluttering programmes. For a second they were arrested in mid-air, as though sheer astonishment held them rigid. Then, as they became even more agitated, he raised his hand in a careless, but singularly graceful, gesture of greeting, before he sat back in his seat again.

"Thank you," whispered Anthea fervently. "Thank you very much indeed!"

"Don't mention it," said Oscar Warrender, with a sort of dry amusement. And then the lights went down for the next act.

Anthea never forgot her first evening at Covent Garden.

For one thing, she had never before, of course, either seen or heard a performance of that standard, and to witness it in the company of Oscar Warrender was a strange and heady experience. Then, to complete an incredible evening, when the opera was over he took her backstage with him, and for the first time Anthea entered that magical world of mysterious illusion and crude reality, of unbelievable drabness and indefinable glamour.

As they went in at the stage door the crowd fell back for him. The doorman greeted him with respect, and people flattened themselves against the wall as he passed. For anyone else she would have found this reaction slightly absurd. For Oscar Warrender, she was bound to admit, it seemed perfectly natural. He was on his own territory and all-powerful.

Even more was she aware of this natural dominion when they went upstairs to the artists' dressing-rooms.

Here she was introduced to the tenor, still in his dark Otello make-up, but remarkably cheerful considering how tragically he had just died; to the charming and courteous Italian who had played Iago with such terrifying and sinister conviction that it was difficult to credit that this was the same man; and finally to the soprano who had sung Desdemona – not, Anthea thought in her secret heart, quite as well as it should have been sung.

Perhaps Oscar Warrender thought so too. At any rate, although the singer chattered to him eagerly in Italian, and called him "Maestro" in every second sentence, he was remarkably non-committal, Anthea noticed.

Then, just as they had come out of the soprano's dressing-room and were preparing to go downstairs again, a striking-looking woman, in a pastel mink jacket which made Anthea gasp, came from the other end of the narrow passage, and they met full face.

"Oscar!" She gave an expressive little laugh, half pleased, half provocative and, to Anthea's astonishment, she reached up and lightly kissed the conductor on his cheek. To her even greater surprise, he smiled and as lightly returned the salute. And, in that moment, Anthea was aware of an extraordinary sensation she had never known before. It was something between anger and pain, and was quite unidentifiable by anything else in her experience.

The conversation was brief, and again in Italian, but it was obvious that they knew each other exceedingly well. He made no attempt to introduce Anthea this time. But she noticed that he laughed and lightly touched the woman's beautiful hand before he moved on.

Anthea followed in his wake, feeling suddenly about fourteen. And although she drew Vicki's golden stole around her, it no longer had the power to make her feel anything but ordinary and rather insignificant.

"This way," he said peremptorily, as they came out of the stage door. And, ignoring two nervously proffered autograph books, he stepped out into the roadway, shepherding Anthea before him. As he did so, a car swept round the corner, driven at high speed, and he snatched her back again out of its path only just in time.

For a moment she was close against him, with his arm round her. And once more the feeling of contact was like an electric shock. It was something so strange and inexplicable to her that she felt almost weak when he released her, and as she walked on she actually stumbled slightly.

"What is it?" He glanced at her in surprise and even put out a hand to steady her. "You weren't scared, were you? There was no real danger, you know."

"N-no, I know there wasn't," she agreed. But, as she walked with him across a corner of the deserted market to where he had parked his car, the conviction came to her that she *had* encountered danger that evening, for perhaps the first time in her life. And the danger had nothing to do with the speeding car.

He seemed disinclined to talk on the drive home, and at first she was silent too. But then, urged on by some compulsion she could not resist, she asked as casually as she could,

"Who was the good-looking woman in the lovely mink jacket?"

"Just now? backstage, you mean? That was Giulia Peroni. Didn't you recognise her?"

"Oh, yes! Now I remember. I have seen photographs of her. I wondered why she seemed familiar. She's very famous, isn't she?"

"She's one of the few artists today to whom one can unhesitatingly apply the word 'great'," he replied.

"Oh." Anthea was both intrigued and vaguely disturbed.

67

And after a moment she asked, "Do you often conduct for her?"

"Almost always when she sings in London, and sometimes when she sings elsewhere too. You shall come and hear her when I next conduct for her. That will be some time next month."

"Oh, thank you! She's – very beautiful, isn't she?"

"No," he said coolly. "She's poised and marvellously intelligent and unpredictably attractive at times, which all adds up to something much more dangerous than beautiful."

He obviously used the word "dangerous" in its most complimentary sense. So Anthea said, "I see," in a rather subdued tone. And after that she was silent until they arrived outside her boarding-house.

Then she thanked him, shyly but fervently, for her wonderful evening. At which he smiled rather drily and said,

"It's all part of your training. Goodnight, Anthea."

She was startled and indescribably flattered that he should use her Christian name. And her answering, "Goodnight," had a happy lilt to it, as she stepped out of the car and ran up the few steps to the front door.

He drove off even before her key was in the lock. But, when she had let herself into the house, she closed the door behind her and leant against it, alone in the dimly lit hall.

"I'm not poised, or marvellously intelligent, or unpredictably attractive," she thought. "And I'm certainly not a bit dangerous. But he called me Anthea!"

And suddenly, because of that, the evening seemed a success.

CHAPTER IV

ANTHEA'S fellow students came in a few minutes later, for as they had to walk some way from the Tube station their journey had naturally taken rather longer than hers.

Immediately she was overwhelmed with laughing thanks for having shared the attentions of her distinguished escort with them, even at a distant remove.

"How did you do it?" Vicki wanted to know. "How did you manage to make him look up at the amphi and actually wave to us? We nearly fainted."

"I just – asked him to," said Anthea.

"Quite simply – like that?" They all laughed incredulously, and Vicki went on insistently, "But what did you *say*? Be a sport and give us a proper blow-by-blow account of things. You couldn't simply have said, 'Those are friends of mine up there; just wave to them, there's a dear.' "

"I didn't say, 'there's a dear'," Anthea assured her with emphasis. But then she laughed, because she recalled the scene with amusement and an extraordinary degree of pleasure. "He didn't really want to do it at first. But then I explained how kind you had all been to me – and he changed his mind."

"Just because you said we'd been kind to you?" repeated Vicki slowly. "He must be very fond of you or something."

"*Fond* of me?" Anthea laughed again at the very notion.

But the idea suddenly came to her, quite unbidden, that it would be somehow breathtaking to have Oscar Warrender fond of one in even the smallest degree. And because of that thought there was the slightest edge to her tone as she said quickly, "Nothing could be further from the case, I assure you."

"Do you mean he doesn't like you?" Vicki looked curious and, to a lesser degree, so did the others.

"I mean that he couldn't be more completely indifferent," Anthea retorted lightly. "He thinks I'm gauche and tiresome and rather stupid. But he does believe I have a voice of quality, and he as good as told me that he would make a singer of me or break me in the process."

"How uncomfortable," said Vicki. "I'm glad I'm no more than mildly talented. It's a hell of a life if you're the real thing. Did he take you round backstage afterwards?"

Anthea nodded.

"What did he think of Otila Franci? – of the Desdemona?"

"Oh, he didn't say!" Anthea was rather shocked at the idea that he might have confided his artistic view to her. "But," she added reflectively, "I had the feeling that he didn't think a great deal of her."

"Quite right of him too," declared several of them in knowledgeable chorus. And Sarah Albany added disparagingly, "She isn't even good second-rate. I bet *he* didn't choose her for the part. Pity we couldn't have had Peroni."

"She's a bit old for it now," Vicki said with a regretful shrug, at which a quite furious argument broke out, first about Peroni's actual age and then about her ability to substitute high art for mere youth.

With an instinct for pouring oil on unexpectedly turbulent waters, Anthea interjected firmly,

"Anyway, she came round backstage. I saw her there."

"Did you *meet* her?" They all stopped arguing immediately and turned to regard her with fresh interest.

"Not actually." Anthea shook her head. "She spoke to Mr. Warrender In fact" – she smiled suddenly – "she kissed him, which I thought rather daring of her. But he seemed to take it rather well."

And, having reduced the incident to an amusing little anecdote, she somehow felt better about it. Particularly as they then all retired to the kitchen to consume cocoa and biscuits which, Vicki informed Anthea, Mrs. McManus always thoughtfully left ready for them if they had been out late.

The following day the new pattern of Anthea's life began to take shape in earnest, and she went for her first singing lesson to Enid Mountjoy, who lived within walking distance.

Although there was great charm and a sort of solid elegance about the handsome house in which the retired singer lived, nothing could have been more different from the flat in Killigrew Mansions. Equally, nothing could have been more different from Oscar Warrender's method of dealing with Anthea.

Anthea knew from the very beginning that she was going to love her lessons with Enid Mountjoy. Not least because she gave full credit to the work already done by Anthea's first teacher, and it was pleasant to know that Miss Sharon's dedicated efforts were appreciated.

"You are not only very gifted," Enid Mountjoy told her. "You have also been exceedingly well taught. And you are essentially musical, which is going to be an enormous help to you. I'm telling you all this quite frankly because I think" – she smiled slightly – "there are probably going to be times when you will require a certain boost to your morale and self-confidence."

71

She naturally made no reference to Oscar Warrender by name, but Anthea gathered that she meant she was not unaware of the special difficulties which might arise from time to time in that direction.

Not that she was anything but a strict and exacting teacher herself. But she had infinite patience and a naturally calm manner, which Anthea was to find, in the next few weeks, a welcome antidote to her stormy sessions with the conductor.

Her language classes were rather fun. And, whatever Oscar Warrender might have said about the poorness of her Italian, she soon found that she had quite a talent for languages, and particularly that she had a good ear for accents.

As for her new home life at Mrs. McManus's boarding-house, Anthea enjoyed every minute of it. It had always been a matter of some regret to her that she had no sister, and in the lively, affectionate and stimulating company of Vicki Donnington she sometimes thought she had found the next best thing.

It was true that Vicki's easy-going approach to her studies differed vitally from Anthea's own wholehearted absorption. But she was so engagingly frank about her own limitations that Anthea was amused, rather than shocked by her attitude.

"Anyway," Vicki explained candidly, "I don't have to make a living out of it eventually. My mother is quite embarrassingly well-off, as it happens. Only she's chosen to marry again and provide me with a stepfather I don't like."

"How awful," said Anthea sympathetically.

"No, no, not really," Vicki assured her. "I don't have to live with them. In fact, it gave me the perfect opportunity of getting away on my own, which was what I really wanted. Mother said plaintively couldn't I *study* something, and as I have a rather pretty voice I said what about studying singing? She thought that was absolutely splendid, as it would take me about two hundred miles away from where she was, and so she provided for me here on a reasonably generous scale, and we're both perfectly satisfied."

"But aren't you and your mother – fond of each other?" asked Anthea, trying – without success – to imagine her own comfortable, commonsense mother behaving in this extraordinary manner.

"Not specially," Vicki admitted, without either rancour or regret. "She's very, very pretty and frightfully young-looking for her age, and I think it embarrasses her to have a grown-up daughter around. For my part, I wish her awfully well, but know we have almost nothing in common. To tell the truth she really bores me dreadfully, and I suppose I bore her just as much, so we're much happier apart."

"I see," said Anthea. But she didn't really see at all. Human relationships in Cromerdale seemed very, very normal in comparison with Vicki's cheerful disclosure.

But, however unconventional Vicki might be in her mother-daughter relationship, there was no doubt that she was a loyal and reliable friend, and Anthea counted her among the happiest features of her new life.

With her singing lessons going well, her language classes yielding good results, and her day-to-day home life gay and pleasant, Anthea could have been supremely happy but for one thing. Only with Oscar Warrender himself did she find it impossible to achieve even meagre success.

It was not that she did not try. Perhaps she even tried too hard. Certainly at times she was so tense and anxious that she could almost hear this reflected in her voice. And then he would growl, "Relax, can't you!" But with a glance of impatient disgust that made it difficult not to exclaim,

"How can I when you look like that?"

She hated him at these times. But she longed for his approval too. She sometimes felt that it would be worth almost anything she possessed just to hear him say she was good. But when she finally wrung his first real expression of approval from him, it was at the expense of so much nerve-strain and anguish that she hardly recognised it as praise.

The whole incident started most unpromisingly, by her being late for her lesson. Or rather, she supposed, when she looked back on the whole incident later, it started with deceptive pleasantness by her being called to the telephone one morning to find Neil Prentiss at the other end of the wire.

"Hello there!" The cheerful familiarity of his voice brought such a wave of joy and homesickness over her that she cried aloud,

"Why, it's Neil Prentiss! How wonderful. Are you speaking from somewhere in London?"

"Yes, indeed. And do you happen to be free for lunch, and willing to take pity on a poor provincial?" he enquired.

"I'd love it!" declared Anthea from her heart. "Do you really mean that you have time for me?"

"I mean that you're the very first person for whom I'm *making* time," he retorted. "I have all sorts of messages from your family, and I've undertaken to bring back all the news of our Cromerdale prima donna. Can you meet me at the Savoy at one o'clock?"

"Rather!" She did not seek to hide her naïve pleasure, and he laughed and said,

"Have you never been there before?"

"No, of course not! I don't go to places like the Savoy."

"Doesn't our worthy conductor ever take you there?" he enquired amusedly.

"Again – of course not. What sort of terms do you suppose we're on?"

"I don't know. Maybe that's one of the things you're going to tell me," was the amused reply. "In the foyer of the Savoy at one o'clock, then."

Not until he had rung off did she remember that her lesson with Oscar Warrender was for two-thirty that afternoon, instead of the more usual three o'clock, and she wished she had warned Neil Prentiss of this. But perhaps he would not mind being hurried a little, and for once she would take a taxi when she left him.

None of it worked out like that at all, however. To begin with, he was a quarter of an hour late. And, although his apologies were profuse and his explanation was more than adequate, she saw her time-limit shrinking drastically.

Anthea explained about her lesson, and he vowed that he would see that she got away in time. And after that she almost forgot the hurrying minutes, because it was so lovely to sit there in the quiet elegance of the Savoy Grill Room and hear him talk about her dear ones at home.

He smiled at her across the table and said, "You've changed quite a lot already."

"In what way?"

"I – don't know." His glance was amused and admiring. "You're more – poised, I suppose. And you look like the kind of girl to whom things happen."

She was charmed. And, although she asked him searching and loving questions about her family and her home town, she thought more than once that he was right. She was now the kind of girl to whom things happened, and in some subtle way she was already rather different from the Anthea who had stood and cried outside Cromerdale Town Hall in the rain.

It was not his fault that it all took very much longer than

either of them had expected. After all, people in a hurry do not go to famous restaurants, where the perfection of the cooking takes precedence over all other considerations. By the end, Anthea was wishing she had insisted on a snack bar.

"I'm sorry it's been such a terrible rush," he said, as she glanced in horror at her watch and refused coffee. "It was entirely my fault. But I shall be in London for a day or two, and perhaps you'll dine with me one evening and we can take things at a more leisurely pace."

"Yes – yes, thank you. I'd love that." She was frantically gathering up her coat and bag. "But I simply must rush now. Do you mind? Will you ring me up?"

"Yes, of course. And I don't mind your running off now. I understand. I'll just stay and settle the bill. And if you have to go before I join you, the commissionaire will get you a taxi." He could not have been kinder or more understanding and, as he held her hand for a moment in farewell, he added with a laugh, "If Oscar Warrender cuts up rough, tell him you were lunching with me."

"Oh, I will!" She was faintly comforted by the thought. For, if Neil Prentiss were providing all her training, even Oscar Warrender could surely hardly complain if she spent a few extra minutes with him.

She almost ran through the great foyer. But she was not the only one wanting a taxi, and there seemed to be some difficulty about getting a specially big American car out of the confined space of the hotel approach.

It was only five minutes really – but five hideously long minutes – before she was in a taxi and on her way. But already Big Ben was chiming the half-hour, and in spite of what Neil had said, Anthea was sick with anxiety.

Rain was falling steadily, and there had been some sort of procession, so that traffic was solid at the entrance to

76

Trafalgar Square, and three times the lights changed colour without any progress being made.

"Can't we go round another way?" cried Anthea desperately.

"What other way?" was the unhelpful reply. And then at last their stream of traffic began to move – slowly, slowly. But at least they were moving.

By the time she finally reached Killigrew Mansions, Anthea was limp, and she simply dared not look at her watch again. Here too, for the first time in her experience, there was quite a long delay while she waited for the lift. And when, at last, she was deposited outside Number Fourteen, her hand was so unsteady that she could hardly press the bell.

The door was opened by a singularly stolid young man, called James Cheetham, who did some coaching at the Opera House and a lot of manuscript copying and other routine work. He already knew Anthea quite well by sight, and he said – unnecessarily, she thought,

"You're pretty late."

"I know." She went past him and into the studio, where Oscar Warrender was sitting at the piano, a little as though he had been waiting there since the moment that she *should* have arrived.

"I said two-thirty," he observed.

"I know. I'm sorry. The traffic –"

"The traffic is no excuse. In London one takes the traffic into consideration. Haven't you discovered that yet? Where were you lunching?"

It sounded perfectly ridiculous, but she had to say, "At the Savoy." And when his eyebrows went up, she added hastily and defensively, "With Neil Prentiss, if you must know. From my home town."

A long pause. Then he said, quite gently,

"If you are ever late again because you have been lunching with some boy-friend from your home town at the Savoy, don't bother to come at all. You will have had your last lesson. Do you understand?"

"Yes, but –"

"There are no 'buts' about this. Either your singing comes first, last and all the time, or I have no interest in you. Is that clear?"

She was shaking with dismay at this reaction, and at the discovery that the name of Neil Prentiss constituted no protection at all.

"I – I can tell you how sorry I am –" she stammered.

"Don't try," he advised her. "It would bore me to distraction. Shall we start?"

She could not possibly be good after that, she told herself. It was all she could do just to get her breath and control her nervous trembling. But he gave her one glance and said, "Pull yourself together," and somehow she did.

"Not very good," was his verdict on the first ten minutes. But then he leaned back and looked at her and said unexpectedly, "Miss Mountjoy tells me she has been trying you out in the last scene of *Otello*."

"Y-yes. I was so thrilled by it that first night that I – wanted to see what I could do with it."

"I see. And what do you think you – did with it?" he enquired drily.

"It isn't for me to say. What did Miss Mountjoy say?" she countered.

"She said your Willow Song and Ave Maria are not without merit," was the thoughtful reply, and he looked at her again in that dangerously considering way.

"I – I'm glad she thinks so," said Anthea, guessing what was coming next, and trying madly to remember everything

78

Enid Mountjoy had taught her about the Willow Song and the Ave Maria.

"I'll hear you," he decided. "Take it from the opening of the scene, when you're first speaking to Emilia. And remember that the fear of death is on you."

She thought few remarks could have been less reassuring in the circumstances. But of course it was true. And somehow she managed to shed her own nervous identity, and take on the chill melancholy of Desdemona, singing her pathetic Willow Song on the last evening of her life.

He let her go right through to the moment between the two arias when Desdemona says goodnight to Emilia. Then he stopped her impatiently and exclaimed,

"No, no! You're not telling her you'll see her in the morning, over the toast and marmalade. You're saying goodbye to her, you little idiot, knowing in your heart that you'll probably never see her again. Listen to these chords" – he struck the terrible fateful chords on the piano – "don't you hear that, as Emilia goes out, death comes in? That's why your cry of farewell should chill the blood. You're afraid – afraid – afraid –"

She felt she was, too, when he said it like that, and stared at her in that cold, inimical way. So she repeated the phrases, and he nodded, presumably satisfied, and let her go on to the long, serene measures of the Ave Maria.

At the end, he let his hands fall on to his knees and asked, "Do you know the rest of the act?"

"Yes, of course."

"Why 'of course'?"

"Because it doesn't interest me to learn an isolated aria or two. I want everything that leads up to and away from them, or I can't get the right mood."

"Good," he said, which nearly knocked her backwards.

And then – "We'll have the rest of the act, then. I'd like to see you act it out."

"But how – without an Otello?"

For answer he went to the door and called, "Cheetham, come here a minute." And when James Cheetham appeared in the doorway he said, "Come and play the last scene of *Otello*. I want to take Miss Benton through it. I'll speak the part."

"From the beginning of the act?" enquired James Cheetham, sitting down at the piano and apparently quite prepared to go through the whole score if necessary.

"No. Just after the Ave Maria. Lie on that sofa, Anthea. You've said your prayers and got into bed and then – Otello comes in."

She did exactly what he told her. But she stared up at him with wide, frightened eyes, as he stood over her, instead of feigning sleep.

"Close your eyes," he said softly. "Close your eyes. You're asleep. And when you open them again, remember that you *love* the man you see there, even though you fear him."

She closed her eyes. She was so much under the spell of his authority that she did not even dare to look at him through her lashes, although that beautiful, flexible speaking voice, saying the words against the sombre background of the accompaniment, had an overwhelmingly terrifying force.

For a moment she thought she could not possibly go on. Then she knew she must. And when she heard her cue from the stolid Mr. Cheetham at the piano, she opened her eyes, leaned up on her elbow and sang her opening notes on a soft rising accent of query.

He was standing looking down at her with heart-searching melancholy as well as indescribable menace, and she suddenly thought of what he had said – "You *love* the man, even though you fear him –"

The conviction was upon her in that moment that this was absolutely true, and, without her even knowing it, there was tenderness as well as terror in her glance, and in her voice too. And then, when he asked her, in tones heavy with fate, if she had said her prayers that night, the whole thing became so chillingly real that all sense of the theatre dropped away from her.

By training and innate discipline the right words and notes came to her, but she cried them out in such tones of terror and pleading that Mr. Cheetham looked over his spectacles in genuine wonder. Then she leapt from the improvised bed, as though really in fear of her life, and would have run right out of the improvised scene if the conductor had not leant forward, snatched her back and flung her on the sofa.

She actually did scream then, and when she felt his hands on her throat she burst into tears.

He let her go immediately, and the piano accompaniment came to a rather ragged stop, while Anthea sat on the sofa, her legs drawn up under her, and cried.

"Stop that nonsense," said Oscar Warrender after a minute. And when it seemed she could not, he sat down beside her and put his arm round her.

"Don't be so silly," he said quietly. "You mustn't be so emotional about it, or we'll never make an artist of you. The feeling has to be there, of course – and you've got loads of that and you're a good girl" – he laughed and lightly kissed the side of her wet cheek – "but you have to master your emotions, and not let them master you. Did I really frighten you so much?"

She nodded without looking up.

"Seems I ought to go on the stage," he observed to James

81

Cheetham amusedly.

"You have a certain talent," agreed that gentleman imperturbably. "But you'd already frightened her a good deal anyway, bully-ragging her about being late."

"I'm sorry."

Anthea looked up then and asked incredulously, "What did you say?"

"It's surprising, I know. But I said I'm sorry." And he gave her that brilliant, rather devilish smile. "I was rather carried away by the scene, I think."

"*You* were?"

"Yes. There's a tribute to your acting." And, with a sharp pat on her cheek, he released her and stood up. "But remember – you must not let your fear and feelings master you."

"I shouldn't with anyone else," she said rather naïvely, at which he laughed not very kindly and replied,

"I shall be no farther away than the orchestra pit, remember, even if I'm not on the stage."

She dried her eyes and looked at him then.

"Do you mean –" she began breathlessly.

"I don't mean anything," he cut in shortly. "I was looking a long way ahead. But if you ever get as far as singing Desdemona on a stage, you can take it I shall be conducting."

"Because you – *want* to conduct for me?" Her lips parted slightly.

"No. Because I have no intention of letting you make a hash of things," was the unkind reply. "But I tell you – that's all a long way in the future. If at all."

She accepted that then, and asked no more questions. But, as she walked part of the way home afterwards through the Park, she thought of all he had said, and it seemed to her that this had been the most fantastic afternoon of her life.

Although the rain had stopped by now, the trees still dripped upon her as she passed. But she was unaware of it. She could think only of that scene in Oscar Warrender's flat, and most particularly when he had said, "Remember you love the man, although you fear him."

"I suppose that's the sort of thing one could say of him too," she thought curiously. "He's simply hateful most of the time. He couldn't have been more odious over my being late. And yet – how he *looked* when he was playing that part. It was only a part, of course – and James Cheetham was right in saying he has a certain stage talent. But it wasn't only that."

She had almost reached the point when she would leave the deserted park and take a bus for the rest of the way, when suddenly recollection hit her like a delayed bomb.

"He kissed me!" she said to the unresponsive, dripping trees. "In a careless, laughing way, he *kissed* me. I never thought of it until this moment. I hardly knew it at the time, but – I remember now. He laughed, I remember, and just touched my cheek with his lips – and said I was a good girl, with lots of feeling."

The recollection gave her the most extraordinary sensation. Something between indignation and acute pleasure. And she thought she understood why Peroni had once said she could kill him – except that she would be a heartbroken mourner at his funeral!

Once more that evening the telephone rang for Anthea, and again it was Neil Prentiss, with kind and rather anxious enquiries about how she had got on at her lesson.

"It was a bit harrowing," Anthea confessed. "He was pretty angry about my being late" – she felt she had better play that down a bit – "but in the end he got over it" – not quite what had happened, of course – "and I had a very exciting lesson."

"How was it exciting?" Neil wanted to know.

"Well, he let me do the last scene of *Otello*, and he played Otello himself and –"

"Does he sing?"

"No, no. He spoke the words. And it follows the play almost exactly at that point, you know."

"Right up to the smothering scene?"

"Yes," said Anthea, rather soberly, because for a moment she re-tasted that moment of terror.

"I don't think that's very suitable," observed Neil seriously. At which Anthea laughed quite immoderately.

"Oscar Warrender doesn't *do* suitable things," she assured him. "But there was nothing offensive about it, if that's what you mean."

"I fail to see how one can be smothered inoffensively," Neil retorted, but he laughed. "What evening have you free for me, Anthea?"

"Why, almost any evening," she told him with pleasure. "I go to the opera sometimes with the other girls. But there's nothing special on this week until Friday, when I'm to go and hear Mr. Warrender conduct for Peroni in *Tosca*."

"Then keep me tomorrow evening, will you? And do you like to go to the theatre or shall we dine and dance?"

"I don't mind. Both sound *wonderful*, and gloriously relaxing."

"Then we'll do both," he replied gaily. "I'll collect you tomorrow about six-thirty, and we'll dine before going to a show. And afterwards we'll go and dance somewhere. Right?"

"A hundred and twenty per cent right!" declared Anthea delightedly. "Thank you so much." When she rang off, she felt that Neil Prentiss was the nicest man in the world.

And then, the next morning, there happened something which confirmed this opinion with almost moving emphasis. Beside her plate at breakfast time was a letter from the firm of solicitors who paid her modest, but adequate, monthly allowance. It contained a money order for two hundred pounds.

"Dear Madam," – stated the letter – "We are instructed by our client to forward you the enclosed money order. Our client feels that, although your lessons, lodgings and general living expenses are covered, there will be legitimate expenses from time to time (clothes for special occasions, etc.) which it might be difficult for you to meet. The enclosed payment of £200 (two hundred pounds) is intended for such purposes, and a similar sum will be remitted to you every other month. Yours faithfully –"

"Oh, it's *too* much," exclaimed Anthea aloud. "He's an angel!"

"Who is?" enquired Vicki, who was the only other person in the dining-room.

"Oh, Vicki," – Anthea looked back at her, almost with tears in her eyes – "I wish I could tell you!"

"Why don't you, then?" suggested Vicki, eating toast with relish and listening with obvious attention.

"Because –" And then suddenly the temptation to share her news with *someone* overcame Anthea completely and, leaning her arms upon the table, she began to tell the whole story.

All about her losing the prize in the television contest by a hair's breadth (she did not mention Oscar Warrender's having talked the others out of giving her the prize) and then how a generous unknown person had come forward and paid for her training.

"But he's not unknown, really. At least not to me," Anthea declared. "There's only one person it could be." And she went on to explain Neil Prentiss's previous kind help to her family, and how everything pointed to his having been her good angel too.

"He must be in love with you," asserted Vicki promptly.

"No, no, he's not," replied Anthea impatiently. "You always think people must be in love with one. I've no time for that sort of thing. I'm going to be an ARTIST. It's just that he thinks very highly of my parents and also believes in my voice and –"

"Is he an old man?" enquired Vicki.

"Old? No, of course not. Why should he be?"

"That's the way you make him sound – attributing all those dull and worthy motives to him. Is he good-looking?"

"Yes. Decidedly."

"Better-looking than Oscar Warrender?"

"I – don't know. I never thought of comparing them. He's much *nicer*-looking than Mr. Warrender. He looks a dear."

"Well, no one's ever accused Oscar Warrender of looking that," Vicki agreed. "Where does the money order come in?"

"Oh –" Anthea glanced down at it as it lay on the table in front of her. Then, since the letter explained itself, she handed this over to Vicki. "You see – it *has* to be Neil Prentiss," she insisted. "He's taking me out this evening, and he guesses I haven't got the right kind of dress for the occasion. That's why he's had the money sent."

"Very close timing," Vicki objected. "Still, it doesn't really matter. The money's the thing! Finish your breakfast and I'll come and help you choose the dress. Have you a class this morning?"

"No. Everything is perfect," Anthea declared.

And so it still seemed to her, later that morning, when, with Vicki's assistance, she chose a gay and enchanting summer evening dress patterned in scarlet and ivory, with a little scarlet jacket to go with it on cool evenings.

"It's a bit extravagant as it's for summer only," Vicki admitted. "But you look a dream in it. And, after all, you must do your Neil proud, since he was so generous"

Anthea thought so too. And any doubts she might have had vanished when he came to collect her that evening. He took both her hands, held her arms wide and looked at her with the utmost approval.

"Absolutely enchanting," he declared. "*That* never came out of Cromerdale."

"Oh, no! I bought it only this morning." She thought he should have the fun of knowing what his gift had done for her. "My ever-generous unknown patron sent me some money and said I was to use it for things like clothes for a special occasion. This," she said, smiling at him, "is a special occasion."

"I feel so too." He laughed in sheer pleasure. "Though I have to break it to you, Anthea, that we shan't have the entire evening to ourselves. Do you mind?"

"No," she said. "Whatever you arrange is all right with me."

"I didn't exactly arrange it." He made a slight face. "At least – yes, I did. But only because I had to. We'll have our dinner and show together. But afterwards I'm afraid I have to play host to a business acquaintance and his wife because –"

"But that's quite all right! I'll go home if you like. After all –"

"No, you won't!" He laughed and drew her arm through his. "I've got you for the evening, and I'm not letting you go. Even if we have to make a foursome of it later, we'll have the best of the evening together first."

And a wonderful evening it was. Anthea thought she had never enjoyed herself more. Over dinner he was a charming and amusing companion, and it seemed that he could not hear enough of her own affairs. He questioned her more closely about what had really happened when she had been late for her lesson, and he was indignantly sympathetic, in a way that was exquisitely soothing after Oscar Warrender's rough handling.

"You don't really need to worry about me," she assured him, as she smiled at him across the table. "I'm beginning to be able to stand up for myself."

He seemed to find that very touching and courageous. So that, by the time they went on to the theatre, Anthea was not only feeling well disposed towards him, but well disposed towards herself too. And there is no subtler compliment that any man can pay a girl.

The play he had chosen was brilliant, and they made the pleasant discovery that the same things amused and interested them both. It was a pity, Anthea could not help thinking, that they were not going to have the whole evening to themselves.

However, the two additions to their party proved remarkably congenial when they joined them later in the famous restaurant of the Gloria Hotel, where Neil had cleverly managed to secure a floor-side table, so that they could either sup or dance as they pleased.

"Like it?" he enquired, looking across at Anthea with that admiring, indulgent air, when the other two had gone to dance.

"I love it! I've never done anything like this before."

She smiled at him radiantly and then looked round, taking in the whole colourful scene. "I don't think I've ever –"

And then she stopped dead. For, threading his way towards them between the tables, came Oscar Warrender, and his expression was grim and uncompromising.

CHAPTER V

"ALLOW me —" Oscar Warrender gave only the briefest nod, in acknowledgment of Neil's presence, and then turned to Anthea and said, in a tone of cold anger,

"What are you doing out at this time of night? You won't be fit for any real work in the morning."

"I have some sort of private life," Anthea began defensively, but Neil came to her assistance immediately.

"Miss Benton is my guest," he explained shortly. "And I take full responsibility for keeping her out late."

"Miss Benton is also my pupil," returned the conductor coolly. "And I take full responsibility for seeing that she goes home at a proper hour. She should be in bed now. Will you take her home or shall I?"

"I — beg your pardon?" Neil looked as though he thought he could not have heard aright. But Anthea knew all too well that he had. She had seen that expression on Oscar Warrender's face before and she knew there was no appeal from whatever he had decided.

She could willingly have struck him at that moment. But she said, with admirable self-control,

"Mr. Prentiss has other guests, and can't very well leave them. And certainly I am not going to have his supper party spoiled. I'll go home myself, as soon as I reasonably can."

"You'll go home now," was the calm retort. "I'll take you myself."

"But I tell you she is my guest," exclaimed Neil.

"And I tell you she is my pupil, and entirely subject to my authority."

"In her private life too?" enquired Neil, raising his eyebrows.

"In everything," was the cold and comprehensive reply.

"I'll go," said Anthea, suppressing her fury with difficulty, and she got to her feet, gathering up her evening bag and her coat as she did so. "Don't worry, Neil. You must look after your other guests. Please make my excuses and explain that I had no option." She gave a cold and angry glance at the conductor, who withstood it admirably. Then to Neil, in a warm and friendly tone, she added, "Thank you. It's been such a lovely evening. We don't want to end it with a scene."

"But I never heard of such behaviour!" protested Neil.

"You'll hear of more like it if you keep in touch with Miss Benton," Oscar Warrender assured him calmly. "Ready, Anthea?"

He had evidently given her all the time he intended her to have for goodbyes. For, with no more than a slight inclination of his head to the angry Neil, he now shepherded Anthea out of the restaurant, through the foyer of the hotel, and out of the swing doors into the street, where his car was waiting.

"I'll take a taxi," she said, standing her ground for a moment and regarding him with unconcealed dislike and anger.

"Get in," he replied, and opened the door of his car. And, since there was no alternative — short of a dispute in the street — she got in. But she stared mutinously ahead as he came round and got into the driving seat beside her. And, as they drove off, she vowed to herself that she would not say one single word to him all the way home.

There was utter silence in the car for a matter of minutes. Then he said impatiently,

"There's no need to sulk. You had to discover, sooner or later, that a singer's life is a strict and dedicated one. Late hours and night-clubs are not for you, and the sooner you learn that fact the better."

She refused to answer.

"And if," he went on coolly, "you fancy yourself in love with that young man, you'd better write that off immediately also. You won't have any time for that sort of thing, I can assure you."

"I think," said Anthea deliberately, "that you're quite the most odious and insufferable person I have ever met."

"Very possibly." He seemed quite unmoved by this expression of opinion. "It's the odious, insufferable people who usually get to the top. The nice, pleasant bores stay in – Cromerdale, for instance."

This time it was she who could hardly believe her ears. Had he no sense of decency at all? There he was, accepting Neil's money for her training, and speaking of him in this contemptuous way. At least, she decided, he should realise that she was aware how atrociously he was behaving, and so she said, coolly and distinctly,

"Do you think it very becoming for you to speak like that of Neil Prentiss when you must be accepting quite a lot of his money for training me?"

There was quite a long pause, during which she hoped he felt as contemptible as she thought him. But when he finally answered, he sounded much more amused than ashamed, she noticed.

"I hadn't really thought of it that way," he said.

"Then think of it now," Anthea retorted coldly. And after that there was silence once more in the car.

When they finally arrived back at the boarding-house,

the conductor took a small envelope from his pocket and held it out to Anthea.

"There's your ticket for Friday night," he informed her. "And mind you're there in good time."

She stared at the envelope without touching it, for in that moment she was loth to accept even so much as a free ticket from him.

"Thank you," she said disdainfully. "But I'll go with the others in the amphitheatre."

"You'll do nothing of the sort," he informed her curtly. "You will sit in the third row of the stalls, where you can appreciate every shade of the performance. It's the first time you've ever heard a great conductor. You may as well be fully aware of what that means."

"Isn't that just a trifle conceited of you?" she enquired drily.

"No, of course not." He remained completely unmoved. "It's an important appraisal of an artist, even though the artist happens to be myself. You will have to learn to do that if you are going to acquire any proper scale of judgment. You'll find that, unless you are able to assess yourself without either coyness or ruthlessness, you will not progress. Take the ticket and stop arguing. It's time you were in bed."

She took the ticket then. But she did not thank him, nor did she bid him goodnight. Why should she? she thought angrily. He gave her the ticket to please himself rather than her, and she did not wish him a good night, anyway. On the contrary, she hoped he would lie awake and think how badly he had behaved that evening. But she very much doubted if he would.

In point of fact, it was Anthea who lay awake, trying to think back over the lovely part of the evening with Neil, but perpetually frustrated by the needling recollection of the way Oscar Warrender had brought the delightful expedition to a close.

"They all say he's a genius," she thought bitterly. "But *I* think his special genius lies in making himself more perfectly odious than anyone else."

And finally, rather pleased with this summing up of the situation, she fell asleep.

The next morning at breakfast, Vicki naturally wanted to know how the evening had gone. So Anthea gave her a glowing account of the play and the supper-party, but without mentioning the intervention of Oscar Warrender.

Vicki, however, was a great one for detail.

"What time did your Neil finally bring you home?" she wanted to know. "And has he arranged to see you again while he's in London?"

Anthea hesitated. Then, because anger surged up afresh within her, she said rather curtly,

"Neil didn't bring me home. Mr. Warrender did."

"Do you mean *he* joined the supper party too?" Vicki's eyes widened and she looked impressed.

"Not quite in the sense you mean," replied Anthea grimly. "He came into the restaurant, saw me there, and took it upon himself to come over and insist on my going home then and there. He lectured me about being out at all at that time of night, saying that a singer's life was a strict and dedicated one – or some such guff. He behaved atrociously," she added, and even now her voice shook with passion as she thought of that scene.

"My dear!" Vicki was enjoyably scandalised. "Didn't your Neil offer to fight him or something?"

"No, of course not. One can't make a scene in public."

"Nor with Oscar Warrender," Vicki added feelingly. "He's the sort of person who says a thing must be, and it's more or less done. No arguments or appeal."

"There was a certain amount of argument."

"But no question of the outcome?"

For a few seconds Anthea did not reply. Then she said, reluctantly, "No question of the outcome."

And suddenly she wished that Neil *had* absolutely refused to let Oscar Warrender take her home, however undesirable or unreasonable that might have been.

Perhaps Neil too felt that he should have been somewhat firmer in his handling of the situation. At any rate, he telephoned before she had finished her breakfast, full of concern and apologies.

"I simply can't get over his insolence," he said. "And I can't tell you how sorry I am, Anthea, that I just could not leave my other guests at that point."

"Please don't worry about it at all." Anthea was immediately warm and reassuring. "I knew you had no choice in the matter. One can't possibly leave one's guest flat. Anyway, when Mr. Warrender is in that mood there's only one thing to do. Obey him."

"I didn't realise that you had quite such a tough time with him." Neil sounded really disturbed. "I'm afraid you must curse whatever well-meaning idiot put you under his direction."

"Oh, no!" Anthea actually laughed in her eagerness to remove any misgiving he might have on that score. "I give my – my unknown benefactor credit for realising that what I wanted above everything else was perfection of training. And certainly I am having that from Oscar Warrender, impossible and odious though he may be. I know I'm lucky to be under him."

"Even though he's so abominable to you?"

"Even so," declared Anthea firmly.

"Well – I don't know." He sounded dissatisfied. "It seems a pretty miserable situation to me."

"Oh, no, Neil!" she cried from her heart. "It's not *miserable*. Nothing as negative as that. Maddening and infuriating perhaps, but extraordinarily stimulating too. I suppose that's why one catches fire."

"*Does* one catch fire for him?"

"Of course."

There was quite a long pause. Then Neil Prentiss said curiously, "All the same, do you rather loathe him, Anthea?"

She opened her lips to say that she did. The words were actually on the tip of her tongue. Then something stronger than her anger held her silent, and suddenly she was confused. Not only in what she should say, but even in what she actually thought. And finally she replied, quite lightly,

"It's a purely professional relationship —" though she knew very well it was not. "Loathing or — or the reverse simply doesn't come into it. He is the man who can make me a singer and, as such, I accept him."

"I see," said Neil. But he sounded puzzled, and Anthea thought she could understand why. She was a good deal puzzled herself on that particular issue.

Neil then explained that he would not be free to see her again that day, but that he had a ticket for the opera the following evening, when he would hope to see her, in one of the intervals.

"And if you can escape from your tyrant," he added, "perhaps we could have supper together afterwards. I'll find somewhere off the beaten track, where he couldn't possibly turn up."

But she said, "Thank you very much, Neil — but no."

"Still scared?"

"Not that. Just that I accept his superior knowledge of what a singer should do."

"I hope he realises what a good pupil he has!"

"I doubt it," Anthea laughed.

"Did he coax or bully you into that state of mind?" Neil wanted to know.

"Neither," said Anthea slowly. "He convinced me by the weight of his natural authority, I suppose."

"Well, well –" Neil sounded half amused, half impatient. "I commend you for your scruples. But I can't help wishing you were a little less conscientious on this occasion."

She laughed at that, but she refused to be moved from her decision. And, having agreed to meet him at the opera the following evening, she rang off.

Later that day, at her singing lesson, Anthea found Enid Mountjoy in a slightly less formal mood than usual, and impulsively she asked her,

"Miss Mountjoy, does Mr. Warrender always behave like a tyrant to his pupils?"

There was a short pause. Then Enid Mountjoy said,

"I don't recall his ever having had another pupil, Anthea, so I don't know."

"N-not ever? Do you mean" – Anthea was astonished, thrilled and rather frightened all at once – "that I'm the *only one* he has ever deigned to take in hand?"

"So far as I know." Her teacher rearranged some scores somewhat unnecessarily on the piano. "It's quite unusual for anyone of his eminence to bother with pupils, you know."

"Then someone – my unknown patron, or whatever I must call him – must be paying him very handsomely to do this," Anthea exclaimed.

"Possibly." For a moment the older woman seemed inclined to leave it at that. Then she added, a little as though

97

she could not help it, "But I doubt if money enters into it much. Oscar Warrender doesn't strike me as exactly hard-up."

"N – no," agreed Anthea, thinking of the flat at Killigrew Mansions. "But then why else, Miss Mountjoy? why else?"

Enid Mountjoy laughed at that.

"Anthea, you're strangely modest for an artist," she remarked amusedly. "Most students would have put forward their own qualities as the explanation long before this."

"You mean" – Anthea looked at her rather shyly – "that he must, somehow, think me good enough to warrant his spending time on me?"

"I think he must, my dear."

"He doesn't give that impression," said Anthea, intrigued but doubtful.

"I'm afraid he is probably a pretty hard taskmaster," the other woman admitted. "But one day you will be glad of that, Anthea. This is almost the hardest life there is, if one does it properly, and perhaps someone has to be hard with us in the very beginning. Kind words and easy applause can come later. Not at the beginning."

"I suppose you're right," Anthea sighed. "But he's pretty beastly sometimes for no reason at all."

"Possibly. All great artists live on their nerves, and seldom suffer fools gladly," replied Enid Mountjoy bracingly. "The general public glibly refers to this as being temperamental. If you have the temperament to put on a great performance, it's asking too much of you that you should go home afterwards and cook the lamb chops with your own little hands. Or, in the case of a man, make yourself tamely agreeable to all and sundry."

"Do you think Mr. Warrender *has* any nerves?" asked Anthea, who had seized on that interesting possibility in preference to anything else that had been said.

"Of course."

"Do you think he's feeling nervous about tomorrow night, for instance?" Anthea was fascinated by the thought.

"Well" – Enid Mountjoy smiled – "I suppose he has conducted *Tosca* often enough not to be exactly jittery about it. But naturally there is nervous tension about *any* evening when the chief responsibility of the performance rests on you. And of course," she added, with good-humoured cynicism, "one always thinks that the chief responsibility rests on oneself."

"Did you ever sing in opera?" Anthea enquired.

"No." The older woman shook her head. "My heart was in it, but the fact that I was lame made it pretty well impossible for me to act on a stage."

"I forgot! I'm so sorry," Anthea exclaimed warmly. "You're so beautifully graceful and dignified that one never thinks of it, somehow."

"Thank you." Enid Mountjoy smiled slightly. "But, as you will find, one has to be active and completely healthy and as strong as a horse to stand up to an operatic career. Some of them may look almost fragile, but they're tough as steel really. And that's what you're going to have to be."

"You make me think I'm really going to succeed when you talk like that," Anthea smiled.

"Of course you are. I can't imagine Oscar Warrender fostering a failure," was the dry reply.

Anthea thought of that several times during the day, with mingled satisfaction and apprehension. Particularly did she think of it the following evening, when she took her seat in the stalls at Covent Garden, and waited – tense with a sort of excited sense of anticipation – for him to come into the orchestra pit.

As the lights went down, he came in so swiftly that he was at the conductor's desk almost before she realised it.

And he cut short the eager applause with a decisive down-beat which brought in the orchestra on the first chords of *Tosca*.

After that, Anthea was away once more in the world of magic, fascinated not only by what was happening on the stage, but also by the extraordinary domination of the man at the conductor's desk.

The almost elemental power and force she had expected. But the subtle balance, the marvellous flexibility and the crystal-clear presentation of the work were quite outside her experience or expectation. She could not have said, of course, by what individual power he achieved his effects. She only knew that it was a performance of radiance and power, of infinite tenderness without false sentiment, of dark menace without bombast.

"It's extraordinary," she heard someone say behind her in the first interval, "how Warrender cleans the score of all the accumulated coarseness and treacly sentiment spread on it by previous conductors, and gives one the work as a new and glorious thing."

"It's a good left hand," replied his companion. "Just watch that left hand."

So, in the second act, Anthea also watched that strong, beautiful, expressive left hand – when she was not breathlessly following the drama on the stage – and she thought she saw what the man behind her had meant. With that secure yet flexible beat of the baton he maintained the form and symmetry of the work, but with his left hand he translated into gesture for his orchestra every nuance of feeling he required of them.

Anthea forgot that she hated him. She forgot that, less than forty-eight hours ago, she had upbraided him contemptuously for criticising Neil. She saw him simply as an overriding genius, who held the threads of a great performance in his hands. And in that moment she almost loved him for the way he could transport her.

In the second interval she found Neil, who also seemed somewhat under the Warrender spell.

"He's an impossible devil," Neil said ruefully, "as one saw all too well the other night. But tonight I take my hat off to him, whereas the other night I could have hit him on the jaw."

"I know what you mean! I've been sitting there thinking more or less the same thing," Anthea confessed.

"Well then, maybe we have to forgive him for being a so-and-so," said Neil was a laugh.

"No. To forgive is something different," Anthea insisted obstinately. "I can't forgive him for some things he has said and done. But I accept them as part of him. I can" – she swallowed slightly – "hate him as a man, but revere him as an artist. The two things are quite different."

"I daresay you're right," Neil agreed amusedly. "Well, keep your flag flying and don't let him bully you too much. Are you still not coming out with me afterwards?"

"No, I mustn't – really."

"Very well. Are you going round backstage to see him?"

"Oh, no, I don't think so."

"Well, in case you do, I'll say goodbye now. I'm going home in the morning." And, bending his head, he kissed her, quite unaffectedly. "Shall I give your love to the family?"

"Oh, indeed, indeed! To all of them. And tell them how I miss them, but that I'm working hard, and I mean they shall be proud of me one day," she said eagerly. "And – and if you should ever think you've guessed who gave me this wonderful chance," she added, on impulse, "tell him – her – whichever it is – that I'll be grateful for the rest of my days, *whatever* Oscar Warrender does to me."

"Darling girl, I will," he promised, smiling into her eyes. And then the warning bell forced them to separate and go to their respective seats.

During the orchestral opening to the third act, she was able to watch the conductor all the time. As she was seated a little to the side, she could see him very well, almost in profile, in the light from the orchestra, and she was reluctantly fascinated by the play of expression on that strong, handsome, faintly arrogant face. And then, just once, at a beautifully executed passage from the woodwind, she saw his quite wonderful smile flash out, and she thought suddenly,

"How he *loves* it all! That's why he can do it with that great romantic sweep. For all his arrogance, he serves the work with everything he has, like a dominating but adoring lover."

It was such an intriguing view of Oscar Warrender — the dominating but adoring lover — that she missed a short passage at that point, and did not come to until the tenor's famous aria.

She had heard this a hundred times before, of course. But it unfolded that night like the petals of a flower, so that she thought she must be hearing it for the first time. And she realised that the talented but slightly brash tenor was being held superbly in check by the conductor, so that everything which was beautiful in his voice was plain to hear, and everything slightly foolish in his approach was disciplined and moulded with infinitely stylish care.

"I could go on my knees to him!" thought Anthea at the end. And she did not mean the tenor. Though, naturally, it was he who got the applause.

At the very end of the performance, as Oscar Warrender turned to go, he sought and found Anthea's glance, and made a slight, imperious sign to her to come round backstage. She faintly resented the form of summons. But she went.

At the stage door she was allowed through without question. Indeed, the man at the door recognised her and said, "Mr. Warrender is in Room One."

So she took her way up to Room One, and knocked rather diffidently on the door.

"Come in," he called. And, when she went in, she found him sitting before the mirror, in a dressing-gown, brushing back his smooth fair hair, his eyes almost glittering with excitement still, although he looked slightly exhausted for once.

"Hello —" he pushed a chair forward for her. "How did you enjoy it?"

"You were wonderful!" She had not meant to say that at all. She had meant to say that the work was shattering, or that Peroni sang superbly. But the other came out without her managing to prevent it.

"A lot you know about it," he retorted amusedly, as he got up and went over to wash his hands. "How well do you think you can assess conducting yet?"

"It's a good left hand. I did discover that," retorted Anthea. At which he turned and came slowly back to her, a towel in his hands.

"How did you know that?" he enquired, in genuine surprise.

"I — I heard someone behind me say so," she admitted, "and so I watched, and I saw it was, too."

He threw back his head and laughed then, so that she thought, "He's almost unfairly handsome." And then he patted her cheek sharply, with his still damp hand and said, "You're learning. What did you think of Peroni?"

"What can one think? She's simply marvellous, isn't she?"

"Yes. She was simply marvellous tonight," he agreed, his deep, expressive voice making the words sound almost like a caress.

"I wonder if he'll ever think *me* marvellous like that?" thought Anthea, with a stab of something like pain.

And at that moment there was a light tap at the door, and Peroni's lovely full voice called, "Maestro, can I come in? Are you decent?"

"Reasonably so," he replied. And, tossing away the towel, he went to the door to admit the heroine of the evening.

She was still in her last act costume, and as she swept into the small room, Anthea got up instinctively and backed against the dressing-table to make way for her.

"My dear" — she actually put both her hands round the conductor's face and reached up to kiss him — "what can I say? You were wonderful tonight."

"*You* were wonderful," he retorted, smiling down at her. "All right. We *both* were." She laughed and put her arms round his neck for a moment. "We're good on our own, but together we are unbeatable. We ought to be together — much more, Oscar."

"We should probably murder each other," he assured her lightly. But he still smiled down at her, and actually touched her cheek, with a half tender, half teasing gesture.

Watching them, Anthea felt devastatingly superfluous. Giulia Peroni still wore, like a shining garment, the fascination and glamour of her performance, and in a curious way Oscar Warrender, too, was like a great stage figure in that moment. For Anthea there was no role except of humble audience — of whom they seemed totally unaware.

In this belief she was wrong, however. He at least did not remain totally unaware of her. He turned, his arm lightly round Peroni, and said,

"I don't think you have met my pupil, Anthea Benton."

"Your – pupil?" Peroni took in Anthea's existence a trifle unwillingly, but she smiled – a beautiful, gracious smile. "I didn't know you had pupils!"

"I don't – usually." But he did not say that it was unheard-of, Anthea noticed.

"Is she specially gifted, then?" Peroni's brilliant glance passed over Anthea again, with a curiosity which was not unfriendly, but was reminiscent of visiting Royalty receiving a small-town official.

"She shows glimmerings of promise occasionally," he replied, before Anthea could even look hopefully expectant. "At other times I think I'm just wasting my time."

"It isn't like you – to waste your time." The singer smiled up at him again.

"No?"

"She is a lucky girl." All the time, she spoke *of* Anthea rather than *to* her. "To be your pupil! My God, what would I have given for such a chance at her age! I suppose" – the smile became rather mischievous – "she adores you?"

"You would have to ask Anthea herself that," was the amused retort.

"Well?" Peroni glanced indulgently at Anthea. "It goes without saying, eh? We work for him – we adore him."

For a second Anthea met the conductor's intensely amused glance, and she saw that he was enjoying her dilemma. Then she replied quite coolly,

"I think, Madame, I am perhaps not the adoring kind. I admire – even revere – Mr. Warrender for his genius. I do not adore him as a person, and I think he would be embarrassed if I did."

"Oh, it takes quite a lot to embarrass me," murmured

105

the conductor, while Peroni laughed, on a not very pleased note, and exclaimed,

"She is cold. You will not make an artist of her if she remains as cold as that, the little one."

"We'll see," he replied calmly. "You shouldn't have pressed her, Giulia. She is truthful — and she doesn't like me."

"Oh — *like*?" The Italian considered the word and rejected it contemptuously. "One doesn't *like* you, *caro mio*. One either loves or hates you. Sometimes both at the same time."

He laughed a good deal at that, and said,

"Well, my beautiful, emotional dynamo, we will leave that question for the moment. Go and change now, or we shall be late for supper."

She made a slightly protesting grimace, but she went. Without, Anthea noticed, bothering to recognise her own existence again.

When the door had closed behind her, he said, "You had better go too, Anthea. It's late enough. And go straight home, mind! No hanging about with your swain from Cromerdale."

"Do you have to make it sound so offensive?" she asked angrily.

He laughed again at that. A good deal seemed to amuse him that evening. And he said, with a wicked glance at her,

"It's an insurance against Peroni's threat. I couldn't have an adoring pupil around, you know."

"You needn't worry!" she flashed out at him. "I don't even like you, as you said. And, if Madame Peroni is right and one either loves or hates you — I know which I do!"

She turned on what she considered a good exit line and would have gone. But, to her astonishment and dismay, he leaned forward and caught her back against him, and she

106

saw, in the mirror opposite, that he was smiling down at her with dangerous brilliance.

"Well, which is it, Anthea?" he said, and for a moment his arms were almost painfully tight around her.

She slowly tipped back her head against his shoulder and looked up at him.

"What do you think?" she demanded, with cool scorn.

"I've sometimes wondered," he replied outrageously. And, bending his head, he kissed her full on her mouth before he let her go.

CHAPTER VI

"How – how dare you do such a thing?" Anthea turned and faced him then, her eyes dark and wide. "I never said you could kiss me. I never intended –"

"Oh, for heaven's sake! Don't be so melodramatic about it," he exclaimed impatiently. And suddenly he was the tired, rather jaded man who had had enough of the evening. "A kiss counts for nothing in the theatre world. There's no need to have heroics. Run along with you – home to your Kensington boarding-house. I'm late already."

She wanted to hurl some verbal thunderbolt at him, to say something – anything – that would make him feel the full weight of her scorn and detestation of him. But he had already turned away from her, and she had the strangely chilling impression that she scarcely existed for him any more.

Shaking with anger, and a sort of dismay which she could neither identify nor explain to herself, she went out of the room. A good many people were clustered in the corridor outside, and some of them glanced at her curiously because she had been allowed to go into the great man's room before them.

But Anthea hardly noticed them, as she made her way past, and then down the stone stairs and along to the stage door.

"Go straight home," he had ordered her, and she had thought that was what she was going to do. But, when she saw the crowd round the stage door, something stronger than her sense of obedience – stronger perhaps than her common sense – checked her. She moved no farther than the fringe of the crowd. And there she waited, in the shadows of Floral Street, until he should come out.

Once or twice, when the night breeze blew chill (as it always does down Floral Street), Anthea thought she should go home. But she could not tear herself away.

She saw the tenor come out, and give autographs to devoted admirers. And then presently there was a concerted surge forward, a chorus of, "There she is!" and a moment later Peroni – radiant and lovely – stood in the doorway, with Oscar Warrender behind her.

He was smiling and obviously in a good mood. And, although Anthea, in safe obscurity, was too far away to hear what was said, she gathered that he made some joke, for the crowd near him roared with laughter, and Peroni gave him a very sparkling glance.

Anthea felt strangely aimless and detached from the scene. Like a child pressing its nose against a shop window to gaze at the Christmas display, without any hope of ever sharing it.

"I can't bear him!" she told herself. "I could have *killed* him when he kissed me in that casual, almost insulting way."

But she still seemed to feel the firm pressure of that strong, arrogant, smiling mouth on hers. And when the couple in the stage-doorway finally made a move to go, and he lightly adjusted the mink wrap round Peroni's beautiful shoulders, she found she was gripping her hands together until they hurt.

They were in the car now, Oscar Warrender in the driving seat, and, as they slowly drew clear of the crowd, Anthea stood there, forgetting everything but the sight of those two, close together in smiling intimacy.

Perhaps she relied too much on the protection of the poor street lighting. Certainly she had not realised how quickly the pattern of individuals in a crowd can shift. As the car moved off, she was suddenly left rather isolated, some way down the street, on the edge of the pavement. And, as the car drew level, he saw her, jerked the car almost to a stand-still and, speaking sternly and distinctly from the half-open window, he said,

"Go home *at once*, Anthea. I don't expect to repeat my orders twice."

Then he drove on, with the smiling Peroni beside him, and Anthea was left standing there, in a street which had suddenly become drab and a little forlorn.

One or two of the diminishing crowd came up to her and someone said, "Lucky you! What did he say to you?"

"He just said goodnight," murmured Anthea.

"Isn't she *lovely*," exclaimed someone else. "They say he's been in love with her for years, and that's why he's never married."

But Anthea had had enough. She pushed her way past the remaining stragglers and made her way to Covent Garden Tube Station. And, on the way home in the train, she found it quite extraordinarily difficult not to cry. Though why she could hardly have said.

No one else was up when she got in, not even the devoted Vicki, and in a mood of inexplicable depression, Anthea went to bed. Or rather, she went to her room and sat on the side of the bed and tried to analyse her own curious re-actions.

"It was a wonderful performance," she told herself. "I

ought to feel elated — by that, if nothing else. Peroni is everything he said she was. She didn't like me, though. I didn't like her, really. Not that that matters."

She got up and began slowly to undress.

"I needn't have made such a fuss about his kissing me, I suppose. He's quite right when he says a kiss means nothing in the theatre world. It didn't mean a thing. Nor did that light kiss he gave me in the studio. Not a thing."

But instead of being reassured by this reflection she felt, if anything, even more dejected.

"One feels so — so *flat*, going home alone," she told herself. "Particularly when other people are going out to supper to enjoy themselves. I wonder where they were going. He didn't say *she* couldn't stay up late. But I suppose when you get to Peroni's position you can allow yourself a few indulgences. She's absurdly possessive about him. Or maybe she kisses everyone in that way. No, I don't think so somehow. Only him. Oh, what does it *matter*, anyway?"

During the next few weeks, Anthea alternated between elation and despair, as she began to take the full measure of the task on which she had started.

In the early days, everything had seemed at least to move forward, even though the sessions with Oscar Warrender had been painful. But now she went through the stage of being unsure of herself. And the more she longed to secure his unqualified approval, the more it seemed to her that this was an impossible goal to attain.

"Don't torment yourself about it," Enid Mountjoy urged her kindly, when Anthea was in the depths of despair one day. "It's always like that with all of us. First one is astonished at the things one learns with comparative ease. Then one is appalled by the things one doesn't know. You're not at all peculiar in this, I assure you. After a while you will

111

gain a sense of proportion and balance the weaknesses against the strengths. You're doing astonishingly well, as a matter of fact."

This, however, did not appear to be Oscar Warrender's view.

He had arranged by now for her to attend some of the rehearsals at the Opera House, but he was cruelly impatient if she failed to draw from them the lessons and conclusions he expected.

"You're amazingly resistant to some of the simplest discoveries," he told her once. "I begin to wonder why I ever bothered about you."

"Because of the money, I suppose," she flung at him angrily.

"What money?"

He looked surprised, and again she realised that he took Neil Prentiss's fantastic generosity almost entirely for granted. Probably, she reflected angrily, he even considered it something of a favour on his part to accept it.

So her tone was very cool as she said, with crude distinctness,

"The very handsome amount of money which I imagine you're being paid for teaching me."

"Oh, that." He shrugged casually, almost disparagingly.

"*You* may forget about it, but I never do. Not one single day. I dislike some of the aspects of my training intensely – and I need not tell you which. But I know it's first-class, and I'll be grateful to my dying day to the man who has given me this chance."

"Very touching," he said. "But hard work and intelligence go much further than a lot of sentimental devotion, you know. Let's go back to what really matters. That's the best way you can show your undying gratitude to the gentleman concerned."

"Why do you dislike Neil so much?" she cried. "You always speak of him in that patronising, disparaging way."

"I?" He looked genuinely surprised again. "I haven't the slightest feeling about your Neil Prentiss, one way or the other. So long as he doesn't distract you from the real purpose of your existence, that is."

"And the real purpose of my existence, in your view, is just to be a singer?"

"Don't say '*Just* to be a singer', in that idiotic way," he retorted, with a sudden and almost violent spurt of anger. "To be a singer – as distinct from a halfwit with a voice – is to have justified your existence, to have answered to heaven for the gifts bestowed upon you, and incidentally to have been touched with the finger of immortality. Now let's get on with the lesson."

So they got on with the lesson.

They sparred incessantly during this period, and sometimes Anthea was almost exhausted by the emotional struggle between them. But, however much he might reduce her to despair between lessons, he always had the power to inspire her and drive her on to further effort when she was actually with him.

"Sometimes," she told Vicki, "I think that if he ordered me to climb up the side of the Opera House, I'd make the attempt, and somehow manage to do it."

"He'll find you something a bit more rewarding than that, I hope," retorted Vicki with a laugh.

"But just as hard," sighed Anthea. And the following day her prophecy was almost dramatically fulfilled.

It was at a rehearsal which she had specially wanted to attend. *Otello* was back in the repertoire, but this time with Oscar Warrender conducting, and she was eager beyond expression to hear him handle this score which fascinated her.

All the morning she sat there in the dark, almost empty Opera House, oblivious of everything and everyone but the people on the stage and the man at the conductor's desk.

She wished passionately that the Desdemona were better, more lyrical and sympathetic. But she supposed sadly that good Desdemonas do not grow on every bush (in which she was perfectly right), and that one had to be satisfied with Ottila Franci, the same, not very satisfactory one she had heard in the performance some weeks ago.

Certainly Oscar Warrender drove the singer to something more than she had achieved on that first evening. But she was, Anthea realised, essentially unmusical, and it became increasingly obvious to Anthea that the conductor's patience was nearing breaking point.

It seemed the singer realised this too, for she became a little wild in her singing, made frequent signs of distress, and finally, just before the last act, she announced that she could not continue.

Everything was against her, she explained volubly. Her throat – she caressed it with an anxious hand. Her head – more gestures to indicate how her poor head was spinning. And her nerves! Her nerves had been too severely tried. And here she directed an angry, half-tearful glance at the conductor's desk.

The other artists stood about the stage rather aimlessly, and the soprano looked over her handkerchief at Oscar Warrender, to see if he would come to heel and plead with her to go on.

He did nothing of the kind, however. Instead, he turned and called into the dark cavern of the empty auditorium,

"Anthea, are you there?"

"Y-yes, Mr. Warrender." She rose from her seat half-way back in the stalls and came hastily down the aisle to him.

"Get up there on that stage and stand in for the last act," he commanded.

"St-stand in?" she gasped. "For the Desdemona, do you mean?"

"I wasn't suggesting you should do Otello," he replied disagreeably. "Hurry, now. We've had enough frustration and delay for one morning."

"But I couldn't possibly do it!" she exclaimed, appalled by the prospect. "I've never even been on a stage before. I –"

"There always has to be a first time."

"But not like this," she pleaded. "With no preparation at all, no chance even to –"

"Do as I tell you," he interrupted harshly, "and don't make so much fuss about it." Then, turning back to the stage, he called up, "I'm sorry you are unwell, signorina. Go home and nurse the sore throat. I'll take the act with a stand-in. Max, are you there?"

The producer, Max Egon, emerged from the wings, looking both worried and intrigued.

"Here's Anthea Benton," Oscar Warrender explained. "She can stand in for the last act. She knows the part and is not entirely impossible."

"Please, please – I can't," whispered Anthea imploringly at his elbow.

He turned and stared at her, with those brilliant, rather frightening eyes.

"You can and you will," he told her brusquely. "Why do you suppose I've been hammering a little artistry and technique into you all this time? Go up on that stage and sing Desdemona. And if you don't do me credit, by God I'll choke you myself, when Otello's done with you."

"Do you think *that's* the way to encourage me?" she said indignantly, and the frightened tears came into her eyes.

And then, by one of those lightning changes of mood, by which he could reduce her to abject submission, he suddenly took her hand in his and smiled at her.

"Do it for me, darling," he said softly. "I need you very badly at this moment."

For a moment she stared back at him. And suddenly the impossible seemed possible, and his fantastic command almost reasonable.

"Very well," she whispered back. "I'll do my best."

And she almost liked the fact that his long, strong fingers closed on hers for a moment until they hurt. Then he released her and, gathering all her reserves of courage, she went from him to the stage, where a half puzzled, half exultant Max Egon was waiting for her.

"Try not to be scared," he said reassuringly to Anthea, as she joined him in the wings. "Remember that everyone is pretty thankful to have you make even a shot at it, otherwise the rehearsal just could not go on."

"But surely," Anthea objected timidly, "there must be a regular understudy for the part? How is it that everything must suddenly depend on me – an absolutely unknown quantity?"

"Because the regular understudy is down with 'flu," explained the producer briefly. "And well did Miss Franci know it! She was really playing up a bit, you know. She hates Warrender because she knows he thinks poorly of her and is a devil for standards. Now come with me and I'll show you one or two stage positions. There's rather little movement in this act, fortunately, and you'll manage all right."

She came out on to the bare stage with him and listened attentively while he paced the distances for her and showed her briefly but tellingly what she had to do and where to place herself.

116

The girl who was singing Emilia smiled at her in a friendly way and said, "I'll help you. And it's only a rehearsal, after all."

"But a rehearsal with Oscar Warrender," thought Anthea, and cast a nervous glance towards the orchestra pit.

He was leaning over to speak to the leader of the orchestra, and she was surprised how well she could see him, in the light from the conductor's desk. She was not quite sure at that moment if she regarded him as a menace or a lifeline.

Then he looked up and called, "Ready?" and everyone scattered, leaving only Anthea and the Emilia on the stage.

For a second such panic overwhelmed her that she nearly rushed from the stage too. But then an innate self-discipline – and the knowledge that several people were depending on her – gave her some courage. And the first notes from the orchestra warned her to be ready.

In something between desperation and supplication, she glanced in the conductor's direction, and again she received that wonderful smile which she had seen him occasionally bestow on others but never, until that day, on herself.

"It's part of his technique for making me do what he wants, and doesn't really mean a thing," she told herself. And then she thought no more of him as a person. Only as the supreme support and inspiration which carried her, almost effortlessly, into her first phrases from an operatic stage.

At first, in her nervousness, she hardly seemed to hear anything. And then, suddenly, the glorious intoxication of singing with full orchestra for the first time was upon her. It seemed as though the whole world opened out before her to limitless horizons, and, as her voice soared into the upper reaches of the opera house, it was as though she soared too – a spirit released from human bondage.

Nothing like it had ever happened to her before, and she was so indescribably elated that she would have forgotten all artistic discipline and control if she had not been held by the iron authority, and yet flexible direction, of the man at the conductor's desk.

She had no idea that several people came to stand in the wings to listen to her, or that Max Egon gripped his hands together, almost as though he were supplicating heaven to let this go on happening. She only knew that, because she derived such strength and confidence from Oscar Warrender, she was singing as she had never sung before; and that everything she had ever felt, learned, or known by instinct was being channelled into this performance.

As the last lingering notes of the Willow Song died away high up in the empty spaces of the theatre, there was an irrepressible burst of applause from the people standing in the wings. But this was immediately silenced by the conductor, whose suddenly terrifying and compelling glance reminded Anthea that her final farewell to Emilia must show she was afraid to the very core of her being.

There were the two fateful chords which gave the mood, and then – she could hardly believe it was her own voice – with full power, yet infinitely musical effect, she cried aloud her anguished farewell.

She received no more than the faintest nod from him, but she knew she had done what he wanted and, in a mood of almost genuine serenity, she fell on her knees to sing the Ave Maria. It was all so easy, somehow. Such a natural expression of the doomed girl's hopes and fears. And, at the end, Anthea felt curiously calm, as Desdemona might have felt calm, having consigned her soul to heaven.

She kicked off her shoes and got into the stage bed and, as Otello stole into the room, she tried – as Oscar Warrender had told her with brutal insistence again and again –

to keep her mind entirely employed with the role, even though she was, for the moment, passive and unoccupied.

The death scene remained a genuinely frightening experience, but not nearly so much as it had been on that afternoon when Oscar Warrender played Otello for her in the studio. Nothing in the tenor's reading of the part even approached the terror and horror of that moment when the conductor had caught her, as she tried to flee, and thrown her on the sofa.

But the final scene went without a hitch and, at the end, there was an outburst of spontaneous applause, this time not quelled by the conductor. Several people came forward to congratulate Anthea, and the tenor actually asked her where she had been hiding all this time.

"I'm just a student," she said shyly. "I – I study with Mr. Warrender. That's how he knew I knew the part."

"It's not just a question of knowing the part," observed the baritone, who had joined them at this point. "You have an innate feeling for it. Something one can neither teach nor learn. Congratulations, signorina."

"Oh, thank you!" Anthea, unused to such approval, could not hide her delight. But there was really only one verdict for which she was waiting with breathless anxiety, and when Oscar Warrender came up on to the stage, she ran to him, with an eagerness she had never shown him before and said,

"Was it – all right?"

He looked at her for a moment as she stood before him, wide-eyed and almost tremulous. Then he calmly took her face between his hands and kissed her.

"Yes," he said. "It was all right." Then he turned to discuss some point with Max Egon, and she just went on standing there, trying not to look as dazed as she felt.

Everyone was dispersing around her now. The orchestra

were putting away their instruments, and the singers scattering to their various dressing-rooms, the stage hands tramping round shifting pieces of scenery. Only Anthea stood there – until she suddenly realised that her usefulness was over and she had better go too.

But, even as she turned to go, the conductor looked over his shoulder and interrupted his conversation with Max Egon to say abruptly,

"Wait a minute, Anthea. You'd better come to lunch with me. I want to talk to you."

So she waited a little longer. And presently he indicated that he was ready, and they went from the Opera House together, he apparently so sunk in thought that he had not so much as a word to throw at her.

Once they were in the car she hoped he might speak in some detail about her performance. At least all the others had seemed to think it merited considerable comment. But it seemed she had to be content with his mere verdict that it had been "all right". That – and the kiss of approval.

In a strange way, it was enough, she thought. She could still feel those strong, beautiful hands round her face, and recall the incredible fact that his kiss had had almost a quality of tenderness about it, so that one had forgotten for a moment how arrogant his mouth really was.

He took her to a quiet, secluded Soho restaurant, where he was obviously very well known, and a respectful but fatherly waiter told them both what they had better choose for lunch. Either the conductor was indifferent, or he trusted to the waiter's experience, for he said with good-humoured impatience,

"Whatever you say, whatever you say. But the young lady's tastes are rather unsophisticated, I believe."

Then, when the waiter had gone, he cleared the table in front of him with a quick gesture of his hand and, leaning

120

his arms on the table, he looked straight across at her and asked,

"How much of Desdemona's part do you know?"

"Why, all of it."

"All of it? I don't just mean are you note-perfect? I mean do you know it in the sense that you could, with some coaching and guidance, project it as a fully integrated role?"

She considered that. Then, firmly quelling the nervous, excited tremors which shook her, she said quietly,

"I know it as a full character study. If you consider that what I did this morning was 'knowing' the part – then I know it all. Does that answer your question?"

He did not reply immediately. He drummed his fingers consideringly on the table while the waiter set their first course before them. Then he seemed inclined to leave the conversation unfinished.

This was too much for Anthea, however. She looked at him boldly and said,

"Why do you ask? Have you – have you some idea of making me do it?"

"I'm trying to decide, Anthea." He had never shown indecision before in all her experience of him. "It's a great temptation to let you do it. Or rather, to insist on your doing it – for I should have to bulldoze my way past considerable opposition first. But the risk is as great as the temptation."

"You mean that you think I might make a hash of it?"

"No, no," he replied impatiently. "If I had the handling of you, the chances are that you would make a minor sensation. That's the risk."

"I don't think I – understand."

"Of course not. How should you?" he rejoined disagreeably. "But if you made a success you would get a great deal of passing publicity. It's the favourite story. Girl springs to fame in a night. Then every opera manager without a conscience — which means most of them — would be eager to exploit you. You would have quite a number of really tempting offers, I assure you. And if you then liked to turn your back on me, having said, 'Thanks, Mr. Warrender, I'm made,' that would be the beginning of three years of cheap success for you — and the end of one of the few good lyric voices I've heard in the last decade."

"And why," asked Anthea quietly, "should you think I would turn my back on you?"

"You don't like me, for one thing." He gave her that quick, wicked, flashing smile. "And I am aware that I am not an easy taskmaster. If you left me, you would be offered star roles — for a while. For my part, I should keep you on small parts, and the good, slightly dull, bread-and-butter roles, where you get no applause for anything but pure singing. Only when your voice is fully 'set' and your vocal discipline perfect would I allow you the dramatic stuff in which you can be allowed to enjoy yourself as an actress because you are completely secure as a singer."

"Then why even suggest that I might sing a performance of Desdemona now?"

"Partly because I should like to hear you do it," he replied coolly, "and it's vocally safe for you, provided I have the guidance of you. But partly also because I know Otilla Franci means to put me in a spot at some time or another. Like you, she doesn't like me. But, unlike you, she has her own way of taking revenge. She will be diplomatically 'ill' at short notice, I feel sure, in the belief that she will spoil my performance."

"But there would be a regular understudy, wouldn't there?"

"And how many first-class Desdemonas do you think

122

there are, wandering round looking for a job?" he rejoined drily. "When I was a boy, Anthea" — she tried to think of him as a boy and failed — "you could have cast any Verdi opera *well* two or three times over, given a few days' notice. Today they're looking with a flashlight all over Europe for a good Verdi soprano. And do you know why?"

She shook her head, her fascinated gaze on him.

"Because every time a talented singer makes a small success, she is hailed as a new Callas, or he is described as a modern Gigli, and the poor creature's half-baked talents are ruthlessly exploited instead of developed. There's a glitter of starlight as the rocket goes up — and then darkness and extinction. There are times when I could weep over it — and people call me a hard man!"

She had never heard him speak like that. She had never seen him look so angrily unhappy before. And for a moment she was silent in sheer astonishment. Then she said gravely,

"Do you want me to make a solemn declaration or something."

"What do you mean?" He raised those rather cynical eyes and stared at her in a not very friendly way.

She smiled and, raising her hand in a mock gesture of taking an oath, she said, "I hereby promise and declare that, whatever the temptations, I shall not leave your direction until you tell me to go."

"My God," he said softly, "you sound as though you really mean that."

"But I do!"

"Even though you think me — what were the words? — the most odious and insufferable person you have ever met?"

"That's beside the point," replied Anthea, thinking of his lips against hers, and immediately rejecting the thought.

123

"You are the one person I trust absolutely from a professional point of view. I know I'm lucky beyond belief that you're even interested in my career. It would take more than a tempting offer from an ignorant manager to make me turn my back on that."

"I see," he said, and he held out his hand to her across the table. She slowly put her hand into his, and he went on, "I shall be no easier to you because of what you have said, and I shall hold you ruthlessly to your bargain. But, if you do what I tell you absolutely in the next few years, I promise you that you will sing eventually almost anything you like in the world."

"I – I think I shall cry, if you talk like that," she declared, half laughing, half serious.

But he made an impatient little gesture and exclaimed,

"Don't do that. Tears bore me. Now I want you to prepare this part – with me and Enid Mountjoy – as though you might be called upon at any moment to sing it with one, possibly two, stage rehearsals. I'll have you on the stage most days in future. Either walking on in the chorus or doing small parts – anything to get you used to the feel of a stage. Even if I never require you to take the part of Desdemona, the experience will be invaluable."

"But if the occasion *does* arise –?" she prompted him breathlessly.

"I think I shall let you take it," he replied coolly.

After that, he refused to talk any more of professional matters, and very soon the lunch was over.

He seemed so little interested in her now that he let her go off home alone, without attempting to offer her a lift in his car. But Anthea did not mind. She wanted to be alone. To walk and walk through the crowded streets, wrapped in the isolation of her own unbelievable reflections.

It had all come so much, much sooner than she could

124

possibly have anticipated. Whatever he might say about keeping her on small roles, reducing her almost to student level for as far ahead as she could calculate, she knew now that her foot was on the very first rung of the ladder. She had sung on Covent Garden stage, with full orchestra, with Oscar Warrender conducting. And the fact that it had been no more than an emergency rehearsal could not take away from the magic of the thought.

"I don't care how much he bullies me," she told herself rashly. "I don't care how many setbacks and disappointments there may be. I *know* now that I can do it – provided he is there."

That was the most curious – perhaps the really disquieting – thought. She needed him, as she needed light and air, food and drink. She could never even have contemplated what she had done that morning unless Oscar Warrender had been there, first to order her harshly to do what he wanted, and then to guide her unerringly through the ordeal.

"What would I do without him?" Anthea asked herself. And she was suddenly alarmed to realise that the question went far beyond the limits of her professional career. That she could not sing successfully without him was not hard to accept. But at that moment she simply could not imagine life without him either.

He might frighten, agitate, anger and appal her. But if she had to go through life without the flashing light of his genius, the exhilarating thunderbolt of his anger or, most incredibly of all, the touch of almost fugitive tenderness which very, very occasionally tugged at her very heart-strings, there would be no point in anything any more.

It was a sobering thought, and Anthea's face was grave as she walked homeward that afternoon.

CHAPTER VII

THE next few weeks proved to be the most strenuous and harrowing of Anthea's life. If she had imagined for one moment that her declaration of loyalty might sweeten the relationship between them, she was lamentably mistaken. He drove her ruthlessly. And, under his direction, even Mountjoy seemed to become a more exacting taskmistress.

Her sessions at the Opera House, when she might have hoped to lose her identity modestly among the chorus and escape his eagle eye, became a fresh kind of ordeal. They were, of course, intensely interesting and held a special fascination for her since they involved her first intensive experience on a stage. But he thought nothing of singling her out and humiliating her in front of the whole company with some cutting comment, and she soon learned that there was not a moment when he was not aware of what she was doing – or not doing.

"It is not necessary to prop up the scenery. It will stand alone, and you are here for other things," he told her sharply once when, weary beyond expression, she had dared to lean against a fairly substantial wall for a moment's support. "How much vitality do you suppose the scene is going to have if everyone is leaning against something?"

"Gosh, you'd think we were building the Pyramids," muttered another girl in the chorus rebelliously. "Everything's there except the whip, and my guess is that he'd use that too if the union would let him."

The idea made Anthea smile faintly. But that also got

her into trouble. For afterwards he told her that if she found reproof amusing, he would not waste his time on that – or anything else connected with her.

"I don't find anything particularly amusing at the moment," she muttered sulkily. "If I did smile, it must have been a complete oversight. You aren't exactly a laughing matter, you know."

To her amazement, he gave her a slight but stinging slap on her cheek for that piece of impertinence. And when she stared at him in furious incredulity, her hand against her suddenly flushed cheek, he said coolly,

"If you don't like my methods, you can go elsewhere."

"Do you *have* to be so beastly about everything?" she demanded in a voice that shook slightly. "Did it never occur to you that you might get better results by being kind occasionally?"

"Never," he assured her. "Fear of the musical director is the beginning of wisdom, so far as the operatic student is concerned. That is my theory, and I act on it."

They seemed to have come a very long way from that rather moving lunchtime conversation. And she now recalled with a good deal of bitterness the charm and near-tenderness he had lavished on her when he momentarily needed her.

But, in spite of her resentment, she put her whole heart into her work, and she was both disappointed and relieved when the first night of *Otello* came without any sign of Signorina Franci relinquishing her role.

Vicki was even more disappointed than Anthea.

"If only she'd break her ankle or something," she wailed, without scruple. "Not her neck or anything final like that, though I never really want to hear her sing again. But just her ankle. Or if she would have a very bad cold – even that would do."

But Ottila Franci, apparently in blooming health, made her entry at the right moment, though with a lack of good basic tone which made Vicki roll her eyes and nudge Anthea significantly.

Both girls were sitting in the conductor's box, to Vicki's unbounded excitement. Oscar Warrender had informed Anthea that he wanted her, easily available, in the house, even though she was not at the moment officially "covering" the part.

"I want to know exactly where to find you," he told her curtly. "You'd better have my box."

"Can I take Vicki too?" Anthea had enquired eagerly.

"Who is Vicki?" he wanted to know, rather disagreeably.

"You remember," cried Anthea reproachfully. "She lent me her golden stole on the very first night I came to the opera with you. You waved to her – in the amphi."

"Did I really?" He seemed reluctant to remember the incident.

But when she said rather naïvely, "We all thought it was extraordinarily nice of you," he laughed suddenly and said,

"All right. Take Vicki with you."

So Vicki went too, and for her the evening was pure bliss. For Anthea it was a wonderful final lesson. Not only did she note exactly where she could improve on the Desdemona's limitations (though, being human, she did this also, of course). She watched every reaction of the other characters on the stage and, above all, she stored in her musical and artistic memory the exact effects which the conductor strove to attain.

"I can do it better than she can," thought Anthea, without vanity and without false modesty. "Mostly because, though I detest him, I know what he's aiming at. She pulls against him all the time."

Anthea read every newspaper criticism avidly the next morning. And, in spite of everything, she could not control a glow of almost personal pride and joy when she read that "Oscar Warrender is unquestionably the conductor of the age", and that "if we are to regard *Otello* as, in many ways, a conductor's opera, we must admit that it was Oscar Warrender's night".

She wondered if this kind of verdict gave him intense pleasure. After all, even the most confident of performers must gloat a little over a favourable criticism.

"Weren't the reviews marvellous?" she said to him, when she went for her lesson the next day.

"Were they?" He looked genuinely indifferent.

"Of course they were! Everyone went overboard for you. Didn't you read them?"

"No." He shook his head without affectation. "I'm a working musician, not a nine days' wonder. I know quite well if I've served the composer faithfully or not. That's all that matters. Remember that, if ever you get to the top."

"I will," promised Anthea solemnly. And she thought how strange it was that he could mingle such real artistic humility with his extraordinary personal arrogance.

Each time a performance of *Otello* loomed up on the current programme, Anthea went through agonies of hope and fear. And then, quite without warning, something happened which put the whole thing momentarily out of her mind.

One rather dull evening, when she had been doing nothing more exciting than wash undies and set her hair, she was called to the telephone for a long-distance call. Immediately a slight flutter of anxiety made her breath quicken, and she was not entirely surprised when Neil Prentiss's voice said,

"I'm sorry, Anthea dear, but I've some not very good news for you. I think you should know that your mother is seriously ill."

"*Mother*?" queried Anthea in consternation. "You mean Father, don't you?"

"No, no. Your father's going along nicely. We got him away to a convalescent home a couple of days ago. But your mother was rushed to hospital this evening with a perforated appendix and –"

"I can't believe it," gasped Anthea. "Mother was *never* ill." And her voice held the forlorn, bewildered note of one to whom Mother had always been a rock of security and strength.

"I know. That's just it." His voice was full of sympathetic understanding. "I'm afraid she had devoted herself so much to your father's care in the last weeks and months that she had no time to notice any disquieting symptoms of her own."

"Oh, poor darling! I should have been there to look after her," exclaimed Anthea remorsefully.

"No, you shouldn't," was the firm reply. "You're busy doing what we all want you to do. But if you could possibly tear yourself away for a day or two –"

"Of course! Neil, tell me. Is it – is it dangerous?"

There was a moment's hesitation. Then he said,

"It's pretty tricky, dear. And, although she would probably be angry with me if she knew I was sending for you, I think she would be terribly glad if you came. In addition, it's rather a lot for young Roland to shoulder his own. And, above all, we simply must keep your father from worrying. Your mother was going to see him on Sunday and –"

"Yes, yes – of course it's essential that I come," she assured him. "I'll come tonight if there's a train –"

"There isn't, I'm afraid, my dear. I've been looking them

130

up. Nothing gets through on this branch line after the six o'clock from London."

"Then I'll come first thing in the morning."

"Good girl! I knew you would," he said approvingly. "I'm thankful you can get away."

"For an emergency like this of course I can get away – from anything," she insisted. "Thank you, thank you, Neil, for all you are doing."

She was trembling a little but quite calm as she replaced the receiver, and stood there considering what she must do. She would have to telephone to Enid Mountjoy to cancel her lesson in the morning, and then she must let Oscar Warrender know that she would not –

A sharp knock at the street door interrupted her reflections and, still absorbed in her anxious thoughts, she went to open the door.

Outside stood Oscar Warrender, and without preamble he said, "I'm glad I found you in. I've got some urgent news for you."

She backed slightly and he entered without waiting to be asked. And when he said impatiently, "Where can we talk?" she rather fascinatedly showed him into the shabby sitting-room which was fortunately empty at that hour.

"I was just going to telephone you," she began.

"Oh?" He turned and looked at her enquiringly. "How did you hear the news?"

"Neil Prentiss rang me." She could not imagine how he also knew, unless Neil had telephoned to him first, in order to smooth the path for her.

"Neil Prentiss?" he repeated, astonished. "What has *he* to do with it?"

"He's pretty well got everything in hand. I can't go to-night, but I'm catching the first train in the morning and –"

"You're not catching any trains in the morning, my girl,"

he informed her grimly. "You're reporting at the Opera House at ten o'clock, and it's an all-day rehearsal for you. You're singing Desdemona on Saturday night and –"

"But I can't!" cried Anthea. "My mother's ill, and –"

"Your mother's ill?' he repeated incredulously. "Your mother's ill? What the hell does that matter? The chance of your life is coming up, and you're going to have to seize it with both hands. And you stand there and tell me your mother is ill. What are you, for heaven's sake? A child playing party charades or a serious artist?"

"My mother is dangerously ill," she said, managing to keep her voice calm with great difficulty. "I'm needed at home and I'm afraid –"

"You're needed here," he told her brutally. "I'm sorry about your mother" – he did not sound in the least sorry – "but I presume the estimable Neil Prentiss has everything in hand, as you say. They must manage without you."

"They can't!"

"They must!" he shouted at her suddenly. "Great heavens, do you suppose we've worked to this point in order to let everything go? Don't you understand even now what it means to be a professional artist? The performance comes first, last and all the time. Understand that now and for the whole of your future. Your entire family can be ill, your husband can have left you for another woman, your house can be on fire, but if you can get on the stage and do a great performance, YOU GO! Is that clear?"

"There's a time when my family must come first, and –"

"There is no such time." Suddenly he caught her by the arm and jerked her close to him, so that she could see that he was actually pale with anger and that his eyes glittered dangerously. "*This* is what you were born for, and everything else in your life must be subordinate to it. It isn't as though you were just any little pip-squeak of a singer. You have the most beautiful lyric voice I've ever heard – though I didn't mean to tell you so yet. If I were a praying man, I'd say you were the answer to my prayers. Do you think I'm going to let you throw away your great chance?"

"The decision rests with me," she managed to say, shaken though she was by the revelation he had flung at her. "You can't command me against –"

"God in heaven, what do you expect me to do?" he demanded. "Plead with you?"

"N-no." She tried to pull free of him, but he held her fast. "I mean that if I go there's nothing you can do about it."

"Oh yes, there is!" He let go of her with a suddenness which made her stagger back, and all at once the violence left him and he spoke almost gently. "If you go, my dear, you go for good. That's my final word. Choose now. You stay and do what I tell you – absolutely. Or you go and don't bother to return. I shall have finished with you."

He even made an expressive gesture, as though wiping the last trace of her identity literally from his hands.

That was what fixed her attention most. It was at his hands she stared as she strove to make her decision. Those clever, beautiful, slightly cruel hands which could make her or break her as an artist. They expressed everything. Strength, authority, even tenderness when he was conducting. And, even as she stared at them, she saw them instinctively turn slightly outwards, in a gesture curiously suggestive of appeal.

It was that gesture which broke her resistance. She had no need even to look at his face. She did not even raise her head as she said, a little huskily,

"All right. You win. I'll stay. What is it you want of me?"

She heard him slowly expel his pent breath in what she

supposed was relief, and his tone was almost normal as he said,

"Report at the Opera House tomorrow at ten. The rest I will decide when I've seen how the full stage rehearsal goes. Go to bed early tonight and see that you get plenty of sleep." It obviously did not occur to him that anxiety might keep one awake. "You'll need all your strength tomorrow."

Then he turned and left her, and she stood there, silent and motionless, until she heard the street door shut firmly, and Vicki came into the room, to say in an awed tone,

"That was Oscar Warrender, wasn't it? I saw him just as I was coming downstairs. What on earth brought him here?"

"He wants me to sing Desdemona on Saturday night –" Anthea began.

But she got no further, for Vicki let out a shriek.

"At the *Garden*, do you mean? I don't believe it! No wonder you look stunned. Wait till I tell the others! We'll all be there in the amphi yelling for you, of course. It's the most exciting thing that's ever happened! How can you be so quiet about it, Anthea?" And then, a little uncertainly, "What's the matter? Are you so terribly scared?"

"No. At least – yes, of course, I'm scared. But it's not that." And then she told Vicki about her mother's illness, and the agonising decision she had had to take. Though she did not describe the exact type of pressure Oscar Warrender had put upon her.

"I'm terribly sorry." Vicki's vivid, usually laughing face looked very solemn. "But it's the only right decision, isn't it? I mean – I suppose your mother made all sorts of sacrifices to get you where you are. You'd be letting her down terribly if you threw your big chance away, just because you couldn't stand the anxiety of being away from her when she was ill."

"Is that how one should look at it?" Anthea stared

134

thoughtfully at the girl who had always seemed rather frivolous and lightweight, in spite of all her warmth and charm. "Perhaps you're wiser than I am, Vicki."

"I don't know about that!" Vicki looked amused, but gratified. "I guess it's easier to see things straight when one isn't personally involved. Now, is there anything I can do for you?"

"Yes. Could you possibly telephone Neil Prentiss for me – I'll give you his number – and explain that I – I can't come tomorrow, after all. I haven't the heart – or perhaps it's the courage – to tell him myself. And I'll probably start crying if I find myself in contact with home again."

"Leave it to me," Vicki told her firmly. And, thankfully, Anthea did.

Evidently Vicki handled the conversation very capably, for when she came to Anthea later, in her room – where she was already deep in her much-thumbed *Otello* score – she reported,

"He says you're not to worry. That everything is under control, and that the thing which will give your mother most strength and incentive to recover will be the thought that you are actually making a Covent Garden debut."

"Thank you, dear." Anthea squeezed her hand gratefully.

"Anything else I can do?" Vicki wanted to know.

"Yes. Could you possibly come with me tomorrow to the rehearsal? It may be an all-day affair. But I think I must have a friend with me, and there's no one I'd rather have than you."

"*Could I come*? Just try to stop me," cried Vicki, radiant at the prospect. "There's nothing I'd like better, and I'll look after you like a maid, friend and dresser all rolled into one. Only – will Mr. Warrender let me come? He's not keen on outsiders at rehearsal, is he?"

"Mr. Warrender is going to have to let you come," retorted Anthea, with a sudden flash of temper. "I'll have my own way in this at least."

"Prima donna already, I see," observed Vicki delightedly.

And, oddly enough, that was almost exactly what Oscar Warrender himself said the next morning, when Anthea presented herself for rehearsal, with Vicki firmly in tow.

"This is Vicki Donnington," she stated coolly, "and she's staying with me throughout the rehearsal. I need her."

The conductor seemed amused, rather than resistant. And Vicki was allowed past – to the dressing-rooms, to the wings, and indeed anywhere she liked during that remarkable rehearsal.

It was an occasion to be talked of in the Opera House for years afterwards. That incredible Thursday when an unknown girl walked into a star role and carried it off with the style, assurance and artistry of an old-stager.

"You *must* have been on the stage before," declared the girl who was playing Emilia. "You couldn't possibly just drop into it lightly like this."

"Oh, there was nothing light about it," Anthea assured her grimly. "I've been more or less battered into it in the studio. And of course being in the chorus for a while has at least given me the feel of the stage."

"That isn't enough in itself." The other girl shook her head. "You must be tremendously gifted too."

"I'd like to think so," Anthea smiled. "But I doubt if more than a quarter of it is inspiration or even dedication. The rest is sheer gruelling discipline."

The other girl looked at her curiously.

"Well," she observed, "there's something to be said for the Warrender method of ceaseless tyranny if this is what it produces in the end."

"Very likely," agreed Anthea drily. But she was really
136

conducting this conversation with no more than one layer of her consciousness. Nothing was entirely real to her that day but the task on which she had embarked.

She knew, as she moved about the stage, exactly from whom she drew her strength and her security. She knew for whom she put out everything she had and was. She knew that this was Oscar Warrender's performance almost as much as it was hers, and that if she achieved success at the performance on Saturday night, she would have ridden to it on the wave of his power and genius.

But she could not find it in herself to say so much as a word of thanks to him, nor to give him one smile of recognition or acknowledgment. At the back of her mind there smouldered all the time the fury and indignation which had swamped her during that shattering scene the previous evening.

Not that he would worry about that, of course. He had no smiles or thanks to waste on her, if it came to that. They exchanged no personal word during the whole of that long stage rehearsal. Only, by some extraordinary communication of spirit, they seemed to understand each other faultlessly, and to fuse their combined talents into a clear flame which lit the performance from beginning to end.

"If she can do this before an actual audience, Saturday night will provide something of a sensation," observed Max Egon at the end of the long rehearsal.

"She will do it," was all Oscar Warrender said, and the implication in his tone was that he would simply not *allow* her to be less than a success.

Then he called Anthea to him and proceeded to give her her instructions for the next forty-eight hours.

"This is the only stage rehearsal we shall be able to have," he informed her. "But you'll manage all right. I want you back here at three-thirty, for work in one of the practice rooms. There are still several things I want to go over with you. Tomorrow you can rest and take everything quietly. On Saturday morning I'll have you at the studio for a final short run-through of any special difficulties."

"Very well," she said, without expression.

"You did well. I suppose you realise that?" He spoke almost impatiently.

"Yes," she agreed. And then she turned away from him and went to look for Vicki, as though there were nothing more important in her schedule than going off casually to lunch with a girl friend.

"That was rather an obvious snub you gave him," Vicki remarked a little reprovingly, as they went out of the stage door together.

"It was meant to be," replied Anthea.

"You don't think it might be wiser to – well, to placate him a little?"

"No."

"If you don't mind my saying so, in the friendliest way possible, you haven't made a success *yet*," observed Vicki, "and you're going to need him rather badly on Saturday night."

Anthea laughed at that and relaxed her obstinate expression. But she added drily, "He needs me rather badly too."

"That's true, of course," Vicki conceded. "Whatever does it feel like, to be necessary to Oscar Warrender?"

The words gave Anthea the most extraordinary sensation, and she blinked her long lashes rather nervously.

"I can't think of it quite in that way," she said hastily. "I'm just the necessary artist to fill a very awkward gap. I'll do it to the best of my ability, for professional integrity as well as personal reasons. But that doesn't mean that I don't reserve the right to dislike him intensely – and to let him know the fact."

"I couldn't," observed Vicki frankly.

"Couldn't what?"

"Dislike him with that obstinate intensity. He may be a tyrant, Anthea, but he's a terribly attractive one."

"Agreed," was the short reply. "But at the moment the tyranny is more in evidence than the attraction. I can't forgive him for being so totally without understanding over – over Mother's illness."

"Perhaps, Anthea, he just couldn't afford to understand," Vicki ventured. "*Someone* had to take a ruthless decision at that moment, you know."

"Well, no one is better fitted to do that than Oscar Warrender," retorted Anthea with a bitter little laugh. "Don't talk of him any more."

So they talked of other things after that.

But the girls were back at the Opera House in good time, and Anthea and the conductor worked intensively until the early evening. Then he said she could go. But, as she turned away, something in her calm, almost indifferent expression seemed to rile him, for he exclaimed,

"There's no need for you to sulk because I had to exert my authority over a purely personal matter."

"I'm not sulking. I'm just not very happy."

"Is the news about your mother very bad?" he asked, reluctantly, she thought.

"It was bad enough last night. I haven't dared to enquire today. I'm – trying not to think too much about her." Anthea's lashes came down, hiding her eyes, and her full, red mouth was suddenly mutinous. "And I don't want to discuss the subject with you, of all people."

"Why me, of all people?" He reproduced her exact tone with sudden impatience.

"Because you haven't a shred of sympathy or real under-

139

standing for anything like this. All you think of is the performance."

"On the contrary," he corrected her shortly, "I have thought quite a lot about this. But the performance had to be my first consideration – that is my supreme responsibility – and I couldn't afford to make easy promises last night until I had seen how you would shape today. Now I can gauge the position exactly and can afford to give you tomorrow free. And that being so, since the last train for Cromerdale has gone –"

"How do you know that?" she asked in astonishment.

"I made it my business to find out," he replied coolly. "And since, as I say, the last train has gone, there's only one thing for it. I'll drive you up there now."

"Drive me to Cromerdale?" she repeated with a gasp. "But it's two hundred miles or more."

"Two hundred and fourteen," he informed her exactly. "So we haven't any time to waste. Go and get your coat. It's time we started."

"Do you – mean that?" She came slowly over until she stood in front of him and, with an effort, she looked up into that clever, rather inscrutable face.

"I'm not in the habit of saying things I don't mean," he replied, a little disagreeably. "Can you start right away?"

"Yes – of course." She knew she ought to thank him – say something in acknowledgment of this extraordinary effort on her behalf. But she simply could not find the words. And after a moment she went from him to her dressing-room to fetch her coat.

Vicki was sitting there, patiently waiting for her, though she was nodding a little over the book she had brought with which to while away the hours.

"Oh" – she sat up as Anthea came into the room – "are you finished at last?"

"Yes. We're finished."

"Then are you coming home now?" Vicki handed her her coat.

"No. I'm going to Cromerdale." Anthea slipped on the coat.

"Going to Cromerdale?" repeated Vicki in consternation. "But you can't! He'll kill you."

"No. He's driving me there himself."

"*He* is? Mr. Warrender?"

Anthea nodded, and the other girl looked stupefied, as well she might, Anthea supposed.

"I – don't understand," said Vicki at last.

"No. I don't understand very well myself," Anthea admitted. "But he said everything had gone well enough for him to be able to let me have tomorrow off. Then he added, in a rather disagreeable sort of way, that as the last train to Cromerdale had gone –"

"How did he know that?" Vicki interjected.

"He'd made it his business to find out," returned Anthea impatiently. "He always makes it his business to find out – everything. And he said that, as the last train had gone, he would drive me up there himself."

"I – say! That was pretty handsome of him, wasn't it? It must be all of two hundred miles," exclaimed Vicki, impressed.

"Two hundred and fourteen. He'd made it his business to find that out too," said Anthea, and she laughed, just a trifle hysterically, because she was tired and overwrought. Then she came and put her arms round Vicki and kissed her and said, "Thank you, darling. I don't know what I would have done without you today."

"But I didn't do anything!" cried Vicki, immeasurably touched and gratified. "I was just sort of – there."

"Yes, that was it," Anthea told her. "You were *there*.

141

Kind and reassuring and normal, in an utterly crazy and wearing day. Thank you. I'll never forget it."

"Well, it isn't a day I'll forget either," replied Vicki, hugging her in return. "And I'm so glad that it's ended with your being able to go to your mother, after all. Give your tyrant a little credit for that, Anthea."

"I'm not in a mood to give credit." Anthea smiled slightly. "I'm in a rather beastly, temperamental mood, I think. Except that I love you, and am grateful to you."

"Well, love him a little too," returned Vicki, laughing mischievously. "He must have had a hell of a day, and deserves his share of gratitude too, if he's prepared to drive you all that way tonight."

"I couldn't do that – in any circumstances," Anthea said seriously.

Then she bade Vicki goodnight and went back to rejoin Oscar Warrender.

CHAPTER VIII

It was very quiet in the car. Neither Anthea nor her companion spoke during those first miles, but she had never been more intensely aware of anyone than she was of the silent, authoritative figure beside her. Then at last she said, reluctantly,

"Thank you for doing this. I am grateful, even if I haven't said much about it."

"Don't thank me. It's the performance I'm concerned about," he replied drily. "If you had been worrying about your mother as well as yourself, I doubt if you would have given of your best. That's why I'm taking the lesser risk of tiring you. The last thing you should really be doing is rushing about the country so close to a vital performance. But, as a calculated risk, it's worth it."

"*Calculated*," she repeated softly but bitterly. "Everything you do is calculated, isn't it?"

"Everything to do with my work – of course. How else do you suppose people get to the top of their profession? By telling themselves brightly that it will be all right on the night? It doesn't work that way, my dear. The artist who is all right on the night is the one who has laid the foundations of that night with months and years of gruelling training and self-discipline. Any fool can be a pleasing amateur, and hundreds of them are. But the one who emerges as the world-shaker is the utterly professional dedicated performer who has brought ceaseless hard work as well as love and thought to the perfecting of God-given talent. Do you know what the greatest operatic director of the century said about that?"

"No. And who was he? — You?" enquired Anthea rather impertinently.

He laughed at that and said, quite good-humouredly, "Not in this case. It was a Viennese, called Clemens Krauss, who knew more about the development of operatic talent than all the opera directors today rolled into one. He used to say, 'Industry without talent is useless. Talent without industry is exasperating. The two together *can* make an artist.' You have the talent. I've driven you to ceaseless industry. And the chances are that I shall make an artist of you. If you call that calculation, I agree. But it's nothing to sneer or sulk about."

There was a long silence. Then she said, "I'm sorry."

"All right." He laughed softly and, unexpectedly taking her hand, he put it under his on the wheel for a few moments, so that she could feel the warm, strong clasp of his fingers. "I know these are difficult days for you. But I'll take you through them safely. Do you believe that?"

"Yes," she said, without hesitation. And in that moment she had the queer feeling that he could almost arrange that there would be good news awaiting her when she reached home.

After a while he released her hand and said, "Relax and rest now. Even sleep if you can. It's been a tiring day."

"For you too," she murmured. "Don't you ever flag?"

"Not if there's work to be done. But if I get sleepy I'll wake you and get you to talk to me. Otherwise, I'll manage."

She supposed afterwards that he must have managed. Because after a while she was not aware of anything any more except that she was comfortable and that there was no

144

need for her to worry since all her affairs were in infinitely capable hands. The hum of the motor was curiously soothing, and presently she slept.

She had no idea that she slipped comfortably to one side until her head rested against his shoulder. Or that once, when a strong passing light shone on her closed eyes, she turned instinctively and half buried her face against him. Nor did she know that, on one of the very few occasions when the car slowed down, he turned his head and glanced, half smilingly, at the bright head against his arm and the soft curve of her cheek.

By the time she stirred and struggled to the surface of consciousness again he was able to say,

"Half an hour more and you'll be home."

"Half an hour?" She sat up and began to tidy her hair, suddenly very conscious of the fact that she had been lying close against him. "I'm sorry. I – I seem to have been propping myself rather thoroughly against you. Didn't I get in the way of your driving?"

"Not really – no."

"But I must have been leaning quite heavily against your arm. Why didn't you shove me away?"

There was a slight pause. Then he said, smiling ahead at the ribbon of road, "I didn't feel like shoving you away."

For some reason or other that made her laugh. Then she yawned and stretched and said, "I had a wonderful sleep."

"Good. That was what you needed."

"Isn't that what *you* need now?"

"I shan't be sorry to see my bed," he conceded.

"Oh, where will you sleep tonight? I'm afraid there's only a very primitive sort of hotel in Cromerdale. If you don't mind things being rather simple, I think we – we –"

"Thank you, but I can't stay. I'll have to drive back tonight."

"*Tonight*? But I thought we were staying until tomorrow."

"You are. And I'm trusting you to catch the midday train tomorrow, so that you will be back in London by early evening, which will give you a long, quiet night in bed. But I'm due in London for an important meeting at ten o'clock tomorrow morning."

"But you'll be dead!" she cried.

"Oh, no, I shan't. I'm virtually indestructible when it comes to doing something I want," he assured her.

"But surely it can't be necessary for you to be in London then."

"Vital," he replied firmly.

"Why?"

"Because the news of your successful rehearsal will have reached Ottila Franci by now, and she will turn up at the Opera House and say she is able to sing Desdemona after all."

"How do you know she will?" asked Anthea aghast.

"Because, my dear, it is my business to know how all of you tick," he replied amusedly. "And that's the way she ticks. I shall forestall her by being there to point out that she opted out of the performance at her own request and, with great difficulty, we found and rehearsed a substitute who is likely to be a sensation. It would be unfair now to throw away all that. I shall, however, express myself as delighted to let her do the next performance."

"Will she be satisfied with that?"

"No, of course not."

"So there will be a row?"

"Probably. Certainly there will be a verbal tussle, for she commands some solid backing about the Opera House."

"And is – is the result of the tussle in any doubt?"

"None whatever," he assured her calmly, as they turned

146

into the main street of Cromerdale. "Where do you want me to drive you first? To your home, to the hospital, or to Neil Prentiss's house?"

She hesitated, glanced at the illuminated face of the Town Hall clock (that Town Hall where he had first walked into her life!) and saw that it was a few minutes after eleven.

"I think – to Neil Prentiss's house," she said. "He's bound to be up, whereas Rollie might be asleep. And – and I'd rather hear any news from Neil than go to the hospital."

So he drove her to the square, pleasant, well-built house on the outskirts of the town, where Neil and his brother lived with their mother.

"I'll wait here in the car, to see if you need to be driven anywhere else," he told her. "I expect you would rather talk to him on your own."

Anthea was not sure that she would. It was like having all her courage and strength drained from her when she got out of the car into the cool night air, and left the aggressive but reassuring presence of Oscar Warrender behind her.

But, when she knocked on the door and heard Neil's familiar voice call to someone, "It's all right. I'll answer it," she felt that perhaps she had come home.

"Anthea!" As he opened the door the light streamed out upon her, and he cried aloud in his delighted surprise. And then, to her inexpressible joy, she saw her young brother come running out into the hall, at the sound of Neil's exclamation.

"Oh, Rollie – oh, Neil! I managed to come!" She almost fell over the threshold into her brother's arms. And then Neil Prentiss hugged her with an almost equal fervour and said – with blessed speed and understanding, and before she could even voice the anxious question,

"It's all right, dear. Your mother came through the op-

147

eration well, and has been holding her own all day. She's not quite out of the wood yet, but everyone is pretty confident and hopeful."

"Oh, I'm so *glad*! So – so grateful to everyone! I don't know what to say – I –"

They had drawn her into the full light of the hall now, smiling at her in sheer pleasure and relief, and Roland was explaining how the Prentisses had kindly insisted on his coming to them while his mother was in hospital.

"They've been wonderful!" He flashed a grateful glance at the older man. "And now that you're here –" Then he stopped suddenly and exclaimed, "But how on earth *are* you here? There isn't any train at this time of night."

"No. Mr. Warrender brought me by road, as soon as the rehearsal was over," explained Anthea, as though that were exactly the way Mr. Warrender usually behaved.

"Drove you all the way from London?" Roland was obviously impressed. While Neil said sceptically,

"Very unlike him, surely? He doesn't usually show such consideration. Do you want us to put him up too, Anthea?"

"No. He has to go straight back. He only waited to see if I needed to be driven anywhere else. The – the hospital or anywhere."

"You don't need him for that," Neil assured her quickly. "I'll drive you anywhere you need to go now. But anyway, there's no question of your going to the hospital tonight. They won't let you see your mother until the morning." And then, as hospitality got the better of natural resentment, he added, "At least won't Warrender come in and have something to eat and drink before he drives back?"

"I'll go and ask him." Anthea turned back to the still open door.

"Shall I go?" Neil offered.

"No, no," she said hastily. "I'll go." And she went quick-

148

ly down the long path to the gate.

It was very dark beyond the wide swathe of light thrown from the open doorway, and it was not until she actually reached the car that she saw him. He was leaning forward, his arms crossed on the steering wheel and his head on his arms, and as far as she could see, he was fast asleep.

"Mr. Warrender," she said softly, through the open window of the car, but he did not stir. And after a moment she put out her hand and touched him. It gave her the most curious sensation to do so and, for some inexplicable reason, she put her hand lightly on his smooth fair head and drew her fingers down until they rested on the back of his neck.

He gave a quick movement then and sat up. For a moment he looked at her with that peculiarly defenceless expression which some people have when they are only half awake. It was something so completely alien from his personality as she knew it that her voice was very gentle as she said,

"I'm sorry I had to wake you. Are you very tired?"

"No. I'm all right now." He frowned slightly, as though rather annoyed at being discovered in a moment of weakness. "Where is the next port of call?"

"You don't have to drive me anywhere else," she assured him. "Neil will look after me now. The news about my mother is quite reassuring and I can see her tomorrow morning. But Neil says — won't you come in and have something to eat and drink before you drive back? Please do." As though reinforcing her plea, she allowed her hand to slide down until it rested on his. "I'll be worried stiff if you start back right away, tired out as you are."

"Will you really?" He glanced down amusedly at the hand on his. "But I don't know that I should come in and take his hospitality, in the circumstances."

"What circumstances?"

149

"Isn't there some rule about not breaking bread with your enemy?" He still looked amused.

"But Neil isn't an *enemy*!" She was shocked at such an idea. "He doesn't really bear you any grudge for the way you behaved that night you took me home, if that's what you mean."

"That wasn't – quite what I meant," he said. But he got out of the car then, a little stiffly, and followed her up the path.

And presently she had the unreal experience of seeing him drink black coffee and eat hastily prepared sandwiches, while Mrs. Prentiss presided hospitably and Roland and Neil saw to her own wants. It was the most extraordinary mingling of the old life and the new. Everything about the pleasant, homely Prentiss household was typical of Cromerdale, the stuff of which almost all her life had been made. And yet the one person in the scene who did not belong to this at all seemed more significant to her than her own brother, hovering affectionately at her elbow.

He stayed no more than half an hour in all, during which time he made himself so charming that Mrs. Prentiss was obviously dazzled, and even Neil appeared to have forgotten their previous unfortunate meeting.

When the time came, he was preparing to escort Oscar Warrender out to his car, but Anthea jumped to her feet and went instead, a little as though she expected him to give her his last orders.

"Be sure you catch that train tomorrow," he said, as they reached the gate. "I'm trusting you, mind."

"I shan't fail," she promised. "And – thank you, even if you did this for the performance only."

She raised her face to his and looked up at him and smiled.

"What's this?" he demanded amusedly. "An invitation to kiss you?"

150

"If you like to take it that way."

"I – like to take it that way," he said slowly. And, taking her in his arms, he bent her back slightly and kissed her hard on her mouth.

"Oh –" she gave a little gasp. "Was – was that also what you call a calculated risk?"

He laughed at that and flicked her cheek with his fingers.

"Ask me after the performance on Saturday," he retorted. Then he got into the car and drove away.

Anthea went slowly back into the house, where the Prentisses were waiting to welcome her into their circle almost literally with open arms. Nothing could have exceeded their kindness. Like Roland, she was evidently expected to make this her home for the time being. And when Mrs. Prentiss finally took her upstairs to the charming room which had been prepared for her, Anthea said, almost with tears,

"I don't know how to thank you. I simply don't know how to thank you all."

"That's all right, my dear." Her hostess smiled kindly at her. "We're very fond of your family, you know. And Neil says you are going to be a famous singer one day, so of course we're only too happy to help towards your peace of mind at a time like this."

"They're wonderful, wonderful people," Anthea told herself, as she lay awake for ten minutes in her comfortable bed. "*They* are the kind of people who really matter. They haven't an unkind thought in their heads, nor a streak of cruelty anywhere in their whole composition."

And yet her thoughts wandered away from them and their comfortable, secure house, out into the night after a car speeding down the M.1. And when she finally fell asleep the sensation she carried with her was the feel of arms which held her with strength rather than tenderness, and lips which were firm and demanding against hers.

151

The next morning her breakfast was brought to her in bed and, even when she got up and came downstairs, she found that everything had been arranged to give her the maximum comfort and relaxation.

Neil had telephoned to the hospital even before Roland departed to school, and had elicited the information that Mrs. Benton had had a good night and that Anthea would be allowed to see her for a short while during the morning.

"You make me feel I'm already having the prima donna treatment," Anthea told Neil with a smile.

"Well, if Saturday night is a success, you'll be entitled to that in future, won't you?" he replied amusedly.

"Oh, indeed no!" She laughed at that. "Mr. Warrender won't allow me to enjoy more than a brief moment of glory, I assure you. It will be back to the studio and the day-to-day discipline for me after that. But" – she smiled reflectively – "I don't really mind. I begin to see the pattern of it all much more clearly."

"Then he's not a beast any more?" suggested Neil, half laughing in his turn.

"Oh, yes, he's a beast all right!" Anthea was in no doubt about that. "But an infinitely clever, rather wonderful beast, really, I suppose."

For some reason or other, Neil seemed to find that answer not very much to his taste, for he frowned and remarked abruptly that it was time they went to the hospital.

He drove her down there, but insisted that she went in alone, so that her mother could enjoy her exclusive company, and Anthea entered the hospital with her heart beating hard.

It was strange to see her mother lying in bed, inactive and languid instead of energetically in charge of the scene. But she looked less frail than Anthea had expected, and her smile was brilliant when she saw her daughter.

"Why, dearie, how did you get here?" she enquired in happy surprise. "I thought you were miles away, preparing for your debut."

"I was," Anthea assured her, as she kissed her. "But the dress rehearsal went well, and Mr. Warrender drove me up late last night, so that I could have a few hours at home."

"He drove you? Himself? Then he's really rather kind and understanding, after all?"

"Well – no, I wouldn't exactly describe him as that," Anthea said. "But he has his moments. Anyway, he's a marvellous teacher and director, and he seems to think me worth a lot of work and trouble. So I have to put up with it if he cracks the whip rather often." And she made an amused little grimace.

Her mother lay and looked at her with loving satisfaction, and a sort of curiosity too, and presently she said,

"You've changed, Anthea."

"Changed, Mother? How do you mean?"

"You don't look at all like the little singing student from Cromerdale now. You look like – like someone to whom life has become a rich and exciting thing."

"Well, I suppose – it has," Anthea conceded slowly.

"Because of your hopes for tomorrow night?"

"Not entirely."

"Because of Oscar Warrender?" asked her mother shrewdly.

"Ye-es. But only in a completely professional way, you understand," said Anthea quickly. "There's nothing personal in our relationship. Nothing at all. I'm just a voice to him. I don't think he even thinks of me as a woman at all."

"And do you," enquired her mother, "ever think of him as a man?"

"No." Again Anthea answered quickly. "Just as a sort of – of elemental force. He's the inspiration which lights the

153

way ahead, and the storm which drives me on."

"Very uncomfortable it sounds," commented her mother, in her most matter-of-fact, Cromerdale manner. "But I see that might be why you look a little dazzled and enchanted and scared all at once."

Then, before Anthea could enquire just what she meant by that, she changed the subject and asked about Roland, and spoke of the wonderful kindness they had received from the Prentisses.

"I don't know what we should have done without them," she exclaimed. "They seem to be the good angels of our lives. How we shall ever repay them I can't imagine. Unless –" she stopped and looked thoughtfully at her daughter.

"Unless what, Mother?"

"Did it ever strike you, Anthea, that it might be Neil Prentiss who made that extraordinarily generous gesture and provided for your training?"

"Yes, often," Anthea said. "In fact, I'm certain it was he. And I hope that one day I'll be able to repay him for all his kindness to this family by justifying his hopes and making him proud of me."

"Well, perhaps that's all he hopes for." Her mother looked quizzical. "Have you ever let him know that you guess? – or attempted to thank him for his generosity?"

"No." Anthea shook her head. "I thought – at least, Miss Sharon thought – that if my benefactor chose to remain unknown, one should respect his or her wishes."

"Oh, that's taking a sense of delicacy too far!" declared Mrs. Benton briskly. "You've been silent quite long enough to pay tribute to anything like that. *I* think you should thank him – and tell him that you know you owe this great chance tomorrow night to his help."

"It's – a tempting thought." Anthea smiled slowly.

"And, since I shall be earning a good fee for the performance, it's perhaps the right time to say that, the moment I can manage for myself, I don't intend to take everything for granted."

Her mother nodded approvingly. And then suddenly Anthea saw that she was beginning to look tired and, even before the nurse came in to warn her, she decided it was time she should go.

She bade her mother a loving goodbye, promised to write reassuringly to her father at his convalescent home, and then went out into the sunshine once more, where Neil was waiting for her.

"I hope I haven't kept you too long!" She smiled at him radiantly, as she slipped into the seat beside him.

"Oh, no. And there's no need to ask what the news is. You look brilliant."

"Yes. She's going on splendidly. Oh, the *relief*!" She drew a long happy sigh. "And now I can concentrate on tomorrow night."

"That's right." He smiled at her affectionately. "There's plenty of time to run you home for coffee before I take you to catch your train."

"Dear Neil! He thinks of everything," she thought. And suddenly she was very happy at the realisation that she was going to be able to put some of her gratitude into words at last.

When they got back to the house Mrs. Prentiss was out shopping, so they had the place to themselves, and it was Neil who made the coffee and carried it through into the sitting-room.

"Do you realise" – she turned to him eagerly, as he set down the tray – "that tomorrow night I shall earn my first fee as a professional singer?"

"Well, yes, I suppose you will." He looked amused. "I

hadn't thought of that side of it."

"I had. And most of all because it gives me the first hope of beginning to repay the tremendous debt I owe to my – my wonderful benefactor. Oh, I accepted it all willingly, and I was grateful beyond description. But I'd be a pretty poor sort of person if I didn't want to repay one day, shouldn't I?"

He did not answer at once, and she repeated rather anxiously, "Shouldn't I?"

"I don't know," he said slowly. "Suppose the giver didn't *want* you to make a return?"

"But I think," Anthea replied, a little pleadingly, "that he would understand my feelings. You – you don't mind my saying this, do you? You understand my point of view, the way I feel about it?"

"Why of course, my dear. I understand absolutely. But –"

"Then I can say it! And I want so terribly to say it now, at this very minute. Thank you, Neil! Thank you, thank you for all you've done. Nothing could ever repay the kindness and the imaginative generosity, but at least you will allow me to –"

"Just a moment." He had actually risen to his feet, as though moved by some powerful emotion. "You've got something badly wrong, Anthea. Have you been supposing that *I* was responsible for all this?"

"Why, of course!" She went suddenly pale. "You – you are, aren't you? Please, please don't deny it, just because you feel –"

"But, darling girl, I must deny it! I'm not the person concerned. I wish I were. I would accept your adorable gratitude only too willingly. But – I can't."

"You mean –" She stared at him aghast, as though still hardly able to take in what he was saying. "You mean it *isn't* you? But then" – she passed the tip of her tongue

156

over suddenly dry lips — "who is it? Who knows enough — cares enough —?"

She stopped and looked at him almost beseechingly. And after a moment, he cleared his throat and said, rather uncomfortably,

"I've always supposed it was Warrender himself."

CHAPTER IX

"OSCAR WARRENDER?" repeated Anthea in utter consternation. "You couldn't possibly think such a thing! *Oscar Warrender* paid for my training? Oh, no – no. It's just not to be thought of. He's not that kind of man."

"Isn't he?" said Neil sombrely. "I should have thought he was."

"What? Generous and romantic?"

"No. Rather made up with the idea of playing God."

"Oh –" That did sound more like him, she was bound to admit, and for a moment she pressed the back of her hand against her lips in fresh dismay. But she simply could not accept even the bare possibility that she could owe everything to the man she detested, and after a moment she exclaimed,

"Why should he even *want* to, Neil? In the beginning he quite despised me. He even saw to it that I lost that competition."

"And, in so doing, left you entirely dependent on whatever he chose to do," replied Neil drily. "He couldn't possibly have thought of a better way of gaining full authority over you. As for his despising you or your voice, I simply don't believe that he ever did either. On the contrary, I think he recognised immediately that you had talent of a quite extraordinary quality –"

He stopped as Anthea gave a sudden exclamation, and she said slowly,

"You remind me – of something he said – when he was so angry with me for wanting to go straight home to Mother, instead of taking on this performance. He said that he thought I had the most beautiful lyric voice he had ever heard."

"There you are!" Neil sounded gloomily triumphant. "He recognized its unique quality, and he was determined that no one but he should handle you. I'm not blaming him for that, but I think he was a bit unscrupulous in the way he arranged things."

"If he really did what you think it was monstrous of him," she cried. "To do me out of my just reward so that I should be dependent on *him*! Oh, but I can't believe it. I still can't entirely believe it wasn't you, Neil. You said something –" she groped frantically in her memory – "something that made me certain it was you. What was it? What was it?"

Neil looked taken aback in his turn then.

"*I* said something? I couldn't have. I never had the slightest intention of claiming –"

"Yes, yes – don't you remember? It was when I first told you of my successful audition in London. You exclaimed, 'So it worked!' And then you looked as though you could have kicked yourself for having said something indiscreet."

"Oh, that?" Neil looked faintly uncomfortable. "Well, I wasn't entirely surprised when Warrender sent for you to go to London. As a matter of fact, I wrote to him after that competition and told him I thought it disgraceful that he had talked the others out of giving you the prize, when you were undoubtedly the most gifted competitor there. And, incidentally, I added that you needed the money badly for your training. To that extent, perhaps, I did set the wheels turning. But anything else was of Warrender's arranging."

"Oh, Neil!" She gave a long, dismayed sigh, as the cer-

159

tainty began to grow upon her that Neil's suspicions were correct.

"Does it matter so much?" he asked kindly.

"Of course it matters! I can't take money from Oscar Warrender. It's inconceivable."

"You were willing to take it from me," he reminded her gently.

"That's quite different," she said simply. "You're a friend."

He took her hand and gave it a grateful squeeze for that. But, as though wishing to be strictly fair, even to Oscar Warrender, he said,

"A generous gesture is a generous gesture, whoever makes it. Can't you look at it that way?"

"No. Because I don't believe it *was* a generous gesture in his case. It couldn't be. He doesn't work that way. It's as you yourself said. He did it because it would give him power over me. Because I should feel forever indebted to him, and so I should have to do whatever he wanted."

"Anthea, it probably wasn't entirely that. Few people act from a single motive, you know. There was probably an element of generosity in it."

But she shook her head obstinately.

"No, there wasn't. That isn't the way he acts. It's the power motive which prompts almost everything he does. He knew that if I owed him my training, my maintenance as a student, even —" she remembered the red and white evening dress and winced — "even some of my clothes, then he could always throw that up at me, and make me feel that I pretty well belonged to him."

"What do you mean by that, exactly?" Neil frowned.

"Oh, nothing *personal*!" She dismissed that idea impatiently. "I'm simply his artistic creation. That's the way he regards me. And in that sense he wants me to be his. So he put me irrevocably in his debt. Don't you see? It would be a debt I could never really repudiate, because he'd not only have made me – he would have *paid* for me too."

"I think you exaggerate," Neil said uneasily.

"You don't know him as I know him," she countered bitterly. "If he's made up his mind about any artistic matter, he'd bulldoze his way over the Archangel Michael to get it."

"Well, I don't know –" began Neil doubtfully. Then suddenly something made him glance at his watch and he exclaimed, "Heavens – the train! Come on. We're going to have to rush for it if you're to catch it and be in London when you promised."

Immediately she was almost panic-stricken. And so strong was the compulsion of Oscar Warrender's authority upon her, even at a distance, that she forgot what they were discussing and cried.

"Oh, let's go! I promised him I would catch that train. I can't imagine what he'll do if I don't."

They ran out to the car together, actually hand in hand, which gave her an odd feeling of comfort. And on the short drive to the station neither of them made any attempt to discuss further the question of who had provided Anthea's training.

There was very little time to spare. Even as she ran on to the platform the train was coming into the station, and Neil wrenched open the door of a compartment and pretty nearly lifted her in.

"Don't worry," he said, as he kissed her goodbye. "Think only about the performance now. Everything else can wait until afterwards. In any case, we may both be quite wrong. It may simply be that he managed to interest some harmless

161

musical patron in you. These things do happen. Forget it! Forget it until the performance is over. Good luck, darling – and bless you."

"Oh, thank you, dear Neil. Thank you for everything." She leaned from the carriage window, and he walked along beside her as the train began to move. "I'll never forget how you comforted and helped me, even if you weren't my unknown benefactor."

He laughed at that and stood and waved as the train gathered speed and she was borne away. Then she drew in her head and pulled up the window. And, as she sank down in her corner seat, she thought that the sight of Neil Prentiss laughing from the platform of dear, safe, familiar Cromerdale station was at least something reassuring to take with her on her journey – to her debut and to her showdown with Oscar Warrender.

Neil's final piece of advice had been good, she knew. The last indulgence she could allow herself at a time like this was an emotional scene, or even a lot of agitating self-questioning. She must try to do what Neil had told her.

It would not be easy. But, for the sake of their vital co-operation tomorrow evening, she would put from her mind any question that Oscar Warrender might have paid for her training, or that he had thrust himself into her life as the benefactor to whom she owed everything.

"We shall have to have a showdown some time. Even quite soon," she told herself. "But not until after tomorrow night. Not until after the performance."

She realised after a while that something of the iron discipline which he had imposed upon her had become second nature to her. For she really did manage to hold back her fears and her anger during that long journey, and she remained in a sort of emotional vacuum. On the one hand she could think with relief and gratitude that her mother was recovering well, and, on the other, that everything had been made as secure as possible for her performance tomorrow night. Those two certainties seemed to cushion her against any sharp awareness of other, more disturbing, factors in her life. And if she owed that security to Oscar Warrender – well, that too she could think of another time.

To her relief and pleasure, Vicki was there at the station to meet her.

"Darling, how did you know what train I would catch?" Anthea hugged her gratefully for the attention.

"Mr. Warrender rang me up" – Vicki was evidently a good deal impressed by the importance thrust upon her on this occasion – "and told me to meet you."

"In order to make sure that I'd caught the train?" enquired Anthea sharply.

"Oh, no. At least, he didn't say anything about that. He said that you would need a good deal of friendly care and unfussy attention just now and that he thought I was the best person to give it to you."

"And so you are!" exclaimed Anthea, ashamed of her momentary sharpness. "It was very kind of you to come, Vicki."

"It was rather nice of him to suggest it too, don't you think?" replied Vicki.

"I – don't know," said Anthea. "I'm beginning to think that I don't really know just why Mr. Warrender does anything."

Vicki glanced at her curiously, but did not question that. Only, when they were seated in the taxi which she insisted on taking, she said,

"He has done some pretty good battling on your behalf, Anthea. I ran into Kate Minden, from the chorus, when I was on my way here, and she says all hell broke loose at the Opera House this morning, because Ottila Franci said she was well enough to sing tomorrow, after all."

"He said she would," murmured Anthea irrepressibly.

"Did he?" Again Vicki glanced at her curiously.

"Yes. That's why he insisted on driving straight back again last night. It must have been dawn before he got in."

"Well, that didn't prevent his being on the spot when Madam created," Vicki observed with relish.

"What happened?" asked Anthea rather fearfully.

"I gather she put her terms, which were that she'd never sing there again if she couldn't have tomorrow night's performance. He let her get that off her chest and then he coolly put his terms. They could dispense with her – or him."

"He didn't!" exclaimed Anthea in horror.

"He did. Of course they didn't either of them mean it," said Vicki indulgently. "But the management knew that if anyone's bluff was called, Oscar Warrender was worth ten Ottila Francis to them. Everyone had a gorgeous time blowing their tops, I suppose. And then he emerged the victor – naturally."

"Naturally," agreed Anthea drily. So drily that Vicki said rather reproachfully,

"He's on your side, you know."

"No." Anthea shook her head. "He's on his own side. He happens to want me in the part tomorrow night, for his own reasons. So Ottila Franci is expendable. If, for any reason, he wanted it otherwise, I assure you I'd be dropped just as ruthlessly."

"Well, I don't know." Vicki looked doubtful. "Most people would crawl on their hands and knees to have Oscar Warrender battle for them like that."

"I am not the kind to crawl on hands and knees for anyone," retorted Anthea disdainfully, as they drew up outside the boarding-house. And Vicki evidently decided to leave the argument there.

164

Everyone, from Mrs. McManus up and down, was very solicitous and affectionate that evening, and Anthea was made to feel a little as though she were made of fine china.

"Don't sit there! There might be a draught, and if you got a cold at this moment –"

"Try a little of this, dear. It'll give you strength and not lie heavy on the stomach. I made it myself, so I know what went into it."

"You'll be making an early night of it tonight. We all did our practising early so that the place would be quiet."

"Would you like –?" "Can we get –?" "Do you feel –?"

"Darlings," said Anthea at last, "I feel disgustingly well and fresh and normal. You mustn't worry about me so much. Everything is going to be fine."

Indeed, if anything, Anthea was calmer than anyone else at Mrs. McManus's boarding-house that evening. And she even slept soundly and refreshingly that night.

But the following morning, when she went to Oscar Warrender's flat for the final run-through, everything which she had feared and suspected the previous day rushed back upon her with renewed force.

She looked into that handsome, determined, faintly enigmatic face and she thought,

"Why did I never suspect the real explanation before? Of course it's just the kind of situation that would appeal to him. Unlimited power – over me and my voice."

Something of her inner stress must have communicated itself to him, for presently he said, with a sort of impatient good humour,

"Relax, child, relax! There's no need to be so tense and scared. I'll get you through tonight safely. Have no fear about that."

"I have no fear about it," she replied. And, oddly enough, that was true. She felt, of course, the natural tremors of stage-fright, the occasional waves of near-panic at the realisation that tonight – *tonight* – she was to make her debut. But she had no deep-rooted fear of failure. She knew, quite simply, that if he said she would be a success, a success she would be.

At the end of the short lesson, in which he had smoothed out the one or two difficulties which had remained after the dress-rehearsal, he closed the score, smiled at her in that half mocking, half indulgent way and said,

"Well, for my part, I'm satisfied. Is there anything left that you want to ask?"

The opening was, though unintended, almost irresistible, and it was all she could do to prevent herself from flinging at him the one query she so desperately wanted answered. But she controlled herself even then and said quietly,

"Nothing, thank you. I think you've covered everything."

Something in her tone seemed still to leave him faintly puzzled, for he frowned slightly. But after a moment he said,

"Very well. Go home now. Rest completely this afternoon. And be at the Opera House by five o'clock."

"I'll be there." She gave a little nod to emphasise that.

"And there's nothing whatever for you to worry about," he told her deliberately. "I've seen to it that you shall have the most experienced person there to make you up, and your dresser probably knows as much about the ways of the house and a performance as I do."

"Quite an admission from you," she said, and smiled faintly and remotely.

"True, nevertheless." Again he gave her that slightly puzzled glance. Then – "I'll come and see you in your room in good time, in case there is anything final to be said, on either side. *Think* yourself into the part of Desdemona – and leave the rest to me."

"Very well," she said, and turned towards the door.

She almost reached it when his voice sounded quietly and authoritatively behind her.

"Anthea, come back here a minute."

She turned immediately and came back until she stood before him, quiet, self-possessed, but with an intangible veil between him and her.

"Look at me," he commanded suddenly.

That did shake her rather. But, after a moment's hesitation, she raised her eyes and looked at him.

When she was close to him like that she could see the fine bone-structure of his face, the faint, clear tan of his skin and the cold brilliance of those alarmingly penetrating eyes.

"We can't leave things quite like this," he said coolly. "What is the matter?"

"Nothing's the matter!" She looked away from him quickly, and then back again as though she could not help it.

"Of course there is," he exclaimed impatiently. "For some reason or other you're an entirely different girl from the one I drove to Cromerdale thirty-six hours ago."

All too true! But she remained obstinately silent.

At that he looked both amused and exasperated, and he said, "Do you want me to coax you or bully you?"

Inexplicably, that was the moment when her resolution broke. Her eyes flashed suddenly and she flung at him bitterly,

"You don't have to do either, do you? After all, you bought the right to command me. Isn't that enough?"

It was a splendid exit line, and she would have turned and gone from him then, but he put out his hand and caught her back against him, just as he had that time in the dressing-room, and all at once she was powerless. Not only because of the strong hands which held her, but because she

167

was suddenly weak at the sensation of being so close against him.

"What do you mean by that, exactly?" he asked coldly. "Stop putting on an act, and talk sensibly for a moment."

"Very well, then, I will! If you want to know, I've discovered who it is who is paying for everything," she cried furiously. "I didn't mean to have it out with you until after the performance. But, since you insist on knowing, you can have the truth now. I know at last that it's *you* who are paying for everything I learn, eat, wear, and am."

"I – see." He had let her go now, and he was suddenly cool and very calm. Even a little remote, in his turn. "I take it you don't – like the situation."

"I loathe it," she retorted, with an emphasis which made even him flicker his lashes slightly. "I see now that it was your way of establishing your absolute authority over me. I could have forgiven you for the bullying and the tyrannising. I could even have forgiven your occasional cruelty. But I'll never forgive you for *buying* your authority over me."

"Do we have to be so melodramatic about it?" he asked disdainfully.

"I'm not being melodramatic. I'm telling you why I can hardly bring myself to be civil to you. If I could walk out on you now –"

"Don't you dare even say it!" He went white with the effort of suppressing his anger and, taking her by both her wrists, he jerked her round to face him. "What you feel or I feel doesn't matter twopence at this moment. Do you understand? Our paltry little affairs count for nothing beside the claims of a great performance. And this can be a great performance tonight. It *will* be. Afterwards" – his voice changed and again he let her go, so abruptly that she stumbled – "afterwards you can tell me exactly what you think of me, if you like. It won't matter then."

"Oh, I shall tell you," she assured him quietly. "Make no mistake about that. I shall tell you."

"But *after* the performance," he warned her. "And perhaps, my temperamental little prima donna from Cromerdale" – suddenly that flashing, almost wicked smile seemed to play around her like lightning – "perhaps I shall then tell you exactly what I think of you."

She stared at him in silence for a moment, half fascinated, half repelled by that extraordinary flame of amusement and confidence. And, even while she told herself that she hated him for finding the occasion somehow funny, she also felt a sort of thankfulness that her fortunes on this vital day rested in the hands of someone so completely sure of himself.

"Go home," he said, almost gently now. "Think only of the performance. Everything else can wait until afterwards."

It was exactly what Neil had said to her. But what had been in him kindly suggestion, in Oscar Warrender was authoritative reassurance.

"Very well." Anthea gave a long, irrepressible sigh. But whether of satisfaction that she had at least let him know that she knew the depths of his infamy, or relief that he was in full command of the situation, she could not have said.

She went from him and out into the sunshine. And, for some inexplicable reason, sudden and complete tranquillity went with her.

CHAPTER X

"You look lovely, dear." The elderly dresser stood back from Anthea, the better to get an overall view of her handiwork. "I must have dressed a dozen Desdemonas in my time, but never one who looked so completely the part."

"Thank you." Anthea smiled shyly. "I hope I can sound the part too."

"Well, that's it, of course! The young ones usually haven't the stamina or the artistry, and the older ones find it difficult to look young and innocent," commented the dresser resignedly. "But from what I heard of the dress rehearsal, you've got both the looks and the voice. No wonder Mr. Warrender's excited."

"Do you think," asked Anthea carefully, "that Mr. Warrender *is* excited?"

"Why, of course. When he came in here a quarter of an hour ago he had that queer sparkle about him that's always there when he senses a great performance coming up. He's like a barometer." The woman bent to pick up a thread, and Anthea gazed down thoughtfully at her experienced grey head. "He measures the operatic pressure like nobody's business," declared the dresser, coming upright again. "If Mr. Warrender says something or someone is going to succeed, then success is in the bag, you mark my words. Well, God bless and good luck. Do you want to sit quietly by yourself until your call comes?"

"Yes, please," said Anthea. And the woman went out of

the dressing-room, and Anthea was left sitting alone before the mirror, trying to still the small tremors which shook her, and unable to believe that the unfamiliar figure in satin and pearls which faced her was her own reflection.

"It's not me, really, of course," she told herself "It's Desdemona. And soon she will have to go out to meet Otello at the entrance of the castle."

As she tried to think herself into the part, she could hear, over the intercom just outside her door, the rustle of a great audience settling themselves in their seat, the occasional cough, the hum of conversation. Then there was a burst of applause, which told her that Oscar Warrender had entered, and a few seconds later the overwhelming music of the Storm and Entrance hit her like a hurricane.

She knew it all so well now that she could visualise every moment. The scene on the stage, though conveyed in sound only, was more real to her than the dressing-room around her. And, even before her call came, she was on her feet and moving towards the door.

In the chill of the stone corridor and steps leading to the wings she felt her courage slipping from her. But the moment she saw the stage the compulsion of the performance was upon her. Just before she made her actual entrance was the worst of all. But then she was on the stage and in the light of the orchestra she could see Oscar Warrender quite clearly, and immediately security enfolded her, and habit and discipline reasserted themselves.

Throughout the act, though she was wholly absorbed in her part of the drama, she was also continually aware of him, and of the fact that she drew both strength and inspiration from him. She might hate him, fear him, quarrel violently with him, but he was her sheet-anchor. And, safe in those strong, magical hands, she sailed triumphantly through to the end of the act.

She received a generous measure of applause and, inexperienced though she was, she could sense the intangible quiver of interest and excitement which emanates from an audience that senses discovery on the horizon.

From the conductor she received no smile – perhaps they were no longer on smiling terms – but he gave her a curt nod which indicated approval, and with that she had to be satisfied.

She rather thought he might come to her in the interval, but he stayed away, and on the whole she was glad of it. She now wanted nothing, either good or bad, to distract her from her work. That he was in the house, and available if she needed him, was enough. For the rest, all personal considerations had fallen away.

The applause for the second act belongs by right to the tenor and baritone, but Anthea also received unmistakably warm appreciation. And after the dramatic and difficult third act there were cheers for her as well as for the other artists. But by that indefinable radar of communication which exists between a sensitive artist and the audience, she knew that they were waiting to judge her fully on her last act. The act which is almost completely Desdemona's.

At one time, such a realisation would have scared her. Tonight it indefinably elated her.

"No over-confidence," she warned herself. "It's one of the biggest challenges in opera. But I can do it. I know I can do it. So long as he is there I can't fail."

And then there was a knock on her door and Max Egon came into the room. The producer was obviously trying not to look worried, and not succeeding very well.

"You're doing splendidly, Anthea," he said heartily. "All set for the last act?"

"Yes, of course. Is – is anything wrong?"

"Well, nothing very seriously wrong. There's been a

slight accident, though, and I think Giles Parry will have to finish the performance for Warrender. But you've worked with him sometimes, and –"

"Finish the performance for Mr. Warrender?" repeated Anthea, absolutely aghast. "But he can't! I can't possibly do it without Mr. Warrender. What's happened? Where is he?"

She pushed past the producer and made for the door.

"Wait a minute," he said quickly. "He isn't dangerously hurt. But he slipped as he came from the orchestra pit just now, and they think he's broken his wrist. The house doctor's there now –"

"Broken his wrist? His *right* wrist?"

"I'm afraid so," Max Egon nodded.

"But then – he *can't* conduct!" She felt suddenly sick, and empty like a stuffed doll that had the sawdust run out of it. "But I can't go on without him. I can't! I must see him!"

She pulled open the door and whirled along the passage to the conductor's room and entered without even knocking.

Oscar Warrender, unusually pale but looking quite calm, was sitting by the dressing-table, and the Opera House doctor was examining his right wrist and forearm. Even as Anthea entered the conductor gritted his teeth and made a rather angry little grimace, and the doctor said,

"Yes, I'm afraid you've cracked the bone, as well as bruising the arm. Can't be absolutely sure without an X-ray. We'd better get you to hospital right away."

"No!" cried Anthea in dismay, from the doorway. "Please – I can't – manage – without you! I can't *do* it with anyone else! I'm frightened. *Do* something!"

She sank on her knees beside the conductor's chair, her lovely stage costume billowing out around her, her face scared and appealing.

"Please don't leave me – now." And suddenly she put

173

her head down against his arm.

The doctor said, "Careful!" But Oscar Warrender said, "Leave her alone." And, shifting himself slightly, he put his left hand on her bright head. It was a compelling rather than a light touch, and his tone was brusque as he said,

"Sit up and stop panicking. I've no intention that anyone else shall conduct for you."

"Oh!" She gave a great gasp of relief. While the doctor exclaimed,

"You can't possibly use that wrist, Mr. Warrender."

"I don't propose to," the conductor replied disagreeably. "I'll have to manage with my left hand. And you, Anthea, will have to be particularly alert, because you won't get exactly the same kind of lead as you're used to."

"I don't mind." She looked up eagerly. "I don't mind, so long as you're *there*. Can you do it? Can you really do it?"

"Yes, of course. Someone get me a brandy. And get up off the floor, Anthea. You're crushing your dress."

Then, to the anxious Manager, who had now come in with one or two other officials of the Opera House, drawn there by the news of the accident, he said,

"Let me have Giles Parry in the pit, in case of emergencies. But I think I can manage."

There was a certain amount of protest. But he overruled everything with the simple, harsh statement,

"I'm conducting this last act. No more discussion."

Anthea just had time to whisper, "Thank you – oh, thank you –" before she was whisked off to take her place on the stage for the rise of the curtain.

In a matter of minutes, it seemed, crisis had dissolved. And though, with one layer of her mind, she was appalled at the nearness of disaster, with another part – and with all her heart – she was ready to sing that last act as never before.

For the first time in all their association, he was going to need her, as well as her needing him. And, with that conviction upon her, she called upon every last ounce of courage and artistry, discipline and inspiration.

And it was exactly as he and she had always intended it should be. There was not a thing she forgot. Her mind was crystal clear, her voice completely at her command, so that she found she could play upon it like a virtuoso string player upon his instrument. And her projection of the innocent, doomed girl took on such a quality of appeal and pathos that Enid Mountjoy – sitting in the hushed and breathless house – was not the only one to wipe away unfamiliar tears.

Far back in some part of her consciousness which had nothing to do with that evening, Anthea knew that there would be other performances in the years to come which would be as fine and secure, as beautiful and possibly as sensational. But tonight it was like being born. Out of the tremendous struggle that had gone before, she was emerging into the world for which God had intended her.

As she buried her face in her hands for a moment at the end of the Ave Maria, the audience paid her the highest compliment any audience can pay an artist. There was a hushed and deathly silence, with everyone so much under the spell of the drama that no one could bear to intrude with applause from the outside world.

She hardly let herself even think of that until the final curtain fell. And then it was as though the silence split open in a rending crash of applause.

The great curtains swept up once more and the Otello – a generous man, as tenors go – led Anthea forward and left her there on the stage alone, while the house shouted its delight. High up in the amphitheatre she heard shrill voices crying "Anthea! Anthea!" and she knew her friends were there and waved, while the rest of the audience applauded afresh.

175

After a while she gave up counting the curtain calls, which she took either alone or in company with the other artists. Then she saw Oscar Warrender – pale and with his fair hair streaked down rather damply – emerge from the opposite side of the stage, to take a solo call and receive his share of rapturous applause.

He stood there smiling slightly for a moment. Then he held out his left hand towards the wings, and someone gave Anthea a friendly push and she went on to join him.

It was the most incredible thing, standing there on the stage of Covent Garden, sharing the thunders of applause with him. And then something even more incredible happened. He turned and kissed the hand he was holding – which provoked another outburst from the sentimental British public – and, under cover of the noise, he said quietly, "Thank you, my darling. You were wonderful."

"*What* did you say?" she whispered, as the curtain fell.

"Just exactly what you thought I said," he replied, as the artists came on to the stage to join them. And then the curtains parted again and there was no chance of further conversation.

He couldn't possibly have said "my darling", of course. That must have been her imagination. But at least he had said she was wonderful. There was nothing more she could ask.

She had forgotten that she hated him. She had forgotten all about owing him money and his having bought his authority over her. She remembered only that she had made her debut and that he had said she was wonderful.

Afterwards, in her dressing-room, she was overwhelmed by congratulations. Several complete strangers kissed her and called her darling. And there were not only telegrams of good wishes but quite a number of flowers. Her friends from the boarding-house had subscribed for a charming bouquet, and there were flowers from Neil Prentiss and her family and the management. There was also a wonderful bunch of red roses with nothing more than "O.W." on the card.

There were her fellow-students, rapturously possessive about her. There was Enid Mountjoy, gravely congratulatory. There was the Manager himself to thank her for her performance, and all sorts of people complimented her and asked her when she was going to sing again.

"I've no idea," she replied in answer to the last question. "It all depends on Mr. Warrender. I don't think he'll let me do much professional work yet. He says I'm still in the student stage."

"Lucky girl," observed one elderly, knowledgeable-looking man. "If Warrender develops you instead of allowing you to be exploited, I don't mind prophesying that we've all heard tonight the debut of a great artist. If, on the other hand, you start singing anything and everything, in the usual way today, you'll last three, possibly four years. Mark my words and accept my congratulations."

Then he took himself off, and someone muttered, "Denton Bloom, you know. Crabbiest but most knowledgeable of all the critics."

It was all exciting and bewildering beyond words. But at last she managed to have the room cleared of everyone except Vicki, to whom she said quickly,

"Go along to Mr. Warrender's room, Vicki dear, and find out what's happened. Tell him I'll be along in a minute, if you see him."

So Vicki, much flown with her sudden importance, went to find out the latest news about the conductor, and Anthea was free to take off her make-up and change.

Vicki was back again before she had finished, with the information that Oscar Warrender was just going off to the

177

emergency ward of the nearest hospital, to have his wrist X-rayed and set.

"I must see him." Anthea wriggled rapidly into her street dress. "I'm going with him."

"I don't think I'd count on that," said Vicki doubtfully.

"Why not?"

"Well, I think Peroni's playing that role," Vicki explained delicately. "After all, she rather considers him her property, doesn't she?"

"Peroni?" Anthea had almost forgotten the famous soprano's existence until that moment. "What's *she* doing here?"

"Fussing round the great Warrender, at the moment. But of course she was in the house during the evening. You don't think she'd let a protégée of his make a debut without her being there to hear for herself, do you? And now she's backstage, pretty well managing everything for him."

"I don't believe it!" Anthea was, inexplicably, both angry and alarmed. "She hasn't any part in tonight's proceedings."

And, brushing past Vicki, she went along once more to the conductor's dressing-room.

He was obviously just leaving, and he looked pale and exhausted. There were already too many people in the room. The Manager and one or two officials of the Opera House, the doctor, and Peroni, looking very lovely and concerned.

For a moment he did not see Anthea. It was Peroni who smiled full at her and said softly and sweetly, "You were excellent, dear. One day you'll make a really good Desdemona."

"Thank you, Madame," replied Anthea, and walked past her to Oscar Warrender. Until she reached him she still had no idea what she was going to say to him. And then her mind went quite blank, and all she could produce was,

"Thank you – for tonight. And – and thank you for my lovely roses."

"Oh, you got them all right?" He smiled slightly and, turning away from the company, seemed to have her for a moment to himself.

"Yes, of course."

"Any comment?" he enquired.

She was puzzled, and a good deal confused by the crowd around them.

"Only – that they're lovely and you chose my favourite flowers."

"I see." Suddenly he looked tired and bored and rather disagreeable. And, because she could not possibly have him look like that, on this night of all nights, she whispered softly,

"Would you like me to come to the hospital with you?"

It was really her olive branch, her way of saying she was friends with him again, whatever hard things they had said to each other that morning. But no olive branch was ever more unceremoniously rejected.

"Good heavens, no," he said impatiently. "Do you think I need you to hold my hand?"

Then he turned back to the room again, and without so much as a "goodnight" to her, he went off with Peroni and the doctor. And there was nothing for Anthea to do but go back to her own room, trying not to look as utterly snubbed as she felt.

Here she found Vicki so full of loving congratulation and happiness that it would have been inconceivable not to try to appear happy too. She *was* happy, of course. Hadn't she just passed through the most wonderful and exciting evening of her life? Was not the bright finger of fame and success beckoning to her? If she could not feel happy and elated tonight, then she never would.

Determinedly, Anthea forced herself to be gay and sparkling. In her dressing-room, at the stage door where she had her first experience of being asked for her autograph, and finally on her way home with her friends from the boarding house – all of them in taxis to mark the importance of this great evening.

Mrs. McManus, who had also, of course, been present in the Opera House to witness her protégée's triumph, had gone on ahead, and when they all arrived a large and appetising supper was awaiting them.

"The time will come, dear, when it will be supper at the Savoy for you after a performance," she prophesied rather emotionally. "But I'll always be proud to say I cooked supper for you on the night of your debut."

"And it's lovely of you to celebrate with *us* tonight, instead of with a lot of notabilities," one of the girls said appreciatively. "I suppose you could have gone out with almost anyone."

"Well, they weren't exactly queueing up to ask me," Anthea replied with a laugh. "And since I can't be with my family, I'd much rather be with all of you than anyone else."

"I suppose you'd have been with Oscar Warrender, if he hadn't had to go to hospital?" Violet Albany said.

"Oh, I don't know." The thought of the smiling, slightly possessive Peroni stabbed her. Then she hastily brushed the recollection aside and said, "I nearly died of fright when I first heard of the accident, and thought he wasn't going to conduct the last act."

"And *we* nearly died of surprise when we saw him pick up his baton with his left hand," declared Vicki. "I must say he was a sport to do it, Anthea. He must have been in a good deal of pain."

"Yes," said Anthea slowly. And for a moment she seemed to feel his hand on her hair and to hear him say, "Leave her alone."

But then she remembered the impatient way he had brushed off her timid overture, when all was over and he no longer needed to keep her calm and happy. And she was silent until Vicki said,

"You got some gorgeous flowers, didn't you?"

"Yes, wonderful. Including yours." Anthea smiled round gratefully on them all.

"Who sent the red roses?" Mrs. McManus wanted to know. "Red roses mean true love, don't they?"

"Well, not in this case," said Anthea drily. "Those are from Oscar Warrender."

"What message did he put on them?" Toni Crann asked curiously.

"Just 'O.W.'," replied Anthea, and without her knowing it, her voice took on a hurt, resentful tone. "It wasn't exactly lavish, was it?"

"Not even 'Good luck' or anything?" Vicki was rather scandalised. "I call that pretty shabby. I spent *ages* trying to think of the nicest thing I could put on ours."

"I'm sure you did. But then you're rather different from Oscar Warrender," Anthea said.

"Well, I can hardly believe it." Vicki actually got up from the table and went to look over the little pile of notes and messages which she and Toni had conscientiously detached from Anthea's flowers before putting them in water. "Yes, you're right. At least –"

She picked out a small square of white and brought it back to the table with her.

"I think there's a card inside that, Anthea. The 'O.W.' is just on the envelope."

181

"What?" Anthea was suddenly alert. "I hadn't realised that!"

And, with more eagerness than she knew, she hastily untwisted the little piece of gold wire which had held the envelope in place and abstracted a card. On it, in small, dark, legible handwriting was:

"It was not my idea to buy authority over you, Anthea. I fell in love with your voice, and I was determined that no one should ruin it. Tonight will be my justification. Oscar Warrender."

"Oh, no!" Suddenly, to the surprise of everyone, Anthea pushed back her chair and rose to her feet. "And I said there was no comment!"

They all stared at her open-mouthed. But she did not even see them. Still clutching the card in her hand, she ran out to the telephone in the hall and, without a moment's hesitation, dialled Oscar Warrender's number.

It seemed that the bell at the other end rang for a long time. Then a voice which she recognized as the housekeeper's said, "Mr. Warrender's apartment. Who is that, please?"

"Is Mr. Warrender back yet?" Anthea's voice was not entirely steady.

"No. He had to go to hospital after the performance. He telephoned a while back, to say he was just leaving there and would stop for something to eat on the way home. Do you want to leave a message?"

"No, thank you." Anthea hung up the receiver, and for a moment she leaned against the wall in the rather dimly lit hall.

"He fell in love with my voice," she repeated in a whisper. "He fell in love – But was it *only* with the voice?"

And suddenly that was the question of all questions in the world that she most needed to have answered. Nothing else mattered. Not fame nor success, not quarrelling nor peace-making. Was it only her voice that he loved? She had to know.

Without any idea of time or place, or of what might seem strange or unseemly, she went back into the dining-room and said,

"Dears, I'm terribly sorry. You must finish supper without me. I have to go out."

"Go *out*?" they cried in chorus. And Vicki added, "But it's well after midnight."

"I can't help that. I have to go. There's – there's something I must clear up."

"But wouldn't the morning do?" asked one of the wind players, a stolid young man who thought twice before he did anything.

"Oh, no – no!" cried Anthea, to whom the thought of waiting even an hour had suddenly become insupportable.

"Where are you going?" enquired Vicki anxiously.

And she hesitated only a moment before she said firmly, "To see Mr. Warrender."

"He'll be furious if you disturb him after a performance," protested Vicki, while Mrs. McManus said, with unexpected primness,

"You can't call on a man at this time of night."

To them both Anthea merely replied, "I can't think about that now." And she reached for her coat, which she had flung off when she came in, and shrugged herself into it.

"At least let us call a taxi for you," said one of the young men. So she waited impatiently for a time while they tried unsuccessfully to telephone for a taxi. Then she exclaimed,

"I can't wait any more. I'll pick up a taxi on the way." And, deaf to all protests – even to those of Vicki, who followed her into the hall, she went out into the night to find the answer to her question.

It was cool and clear outside, with bright starlight over-

183

head, and, as she walked rapidly along, it seemed to Anthea that, ever since she had first seen Oscar Warrender at Cromerdale Town Hall and heard him dismiss her contemptuously as no more than good material, she had been working up to this moment.

"That was what I couldn't take, even then," she thought. "And that's what I've found unforgivable ever since. I was only a voice to him. Or was I?"

She walked for ten minutes before she picked up a cruising taxi. And, when she had given her directions and sunk down in its musty interior, she seemed to regain some sense of reality, which made her ask herself dismayedly what she really thought she was doing.

When she got to his flat, what was she to say to the housekeeper? How could she demand to be let in and allowed to wait at this time of night? Could she say he was expecting her? But, again at this time of night, what sort of impression would that create?

When she reached her destination she was already cold with indecision. But she simply could not go back now. So she paid off the taxi and, as she went up in the lift, she rehearsed some plausible words for the housekeeper.

When she pressed the bell, her hand was shaking a little, as it had that very first time. But she somehow composed her features into a matter-of-fact smile, to accompany the reasonable opening sentence she had prepared.

Neither was required, however. For it was not the housekeeper who opened the door. It was Oscar Warrender himself, in a dark, rather magnificent-looking dressing-gown.

"Anthea!" For once in her life she saw him completely at a loss. "What on earth do you want at this time of night, child?"

"To – to come in, please. If – if I may," she stammered.

"Well, of course." He stood back to allow her to pass and, from force of habit, she went through to the studio. He followed her more slowly, switching on a few extra lights as he came.

Then he stood and regarded her, with a touch of hostility, even wariness, and asked abruptly, "What's the matter?"

"It's about – the note on your flowers," she blurted out, because she had nothing prepared to say to him. Only something to say to the housekeeper.

"Oh – yes?"

"I hadn't found it when you asked me if I – if I had any comment." She stood there clasping and unclasping her hands nervously. "I saw only the envelope. I thought you put only your initials on the flowers. And – and when you asked me, I didn't see what comment I could make."

"I see." The very faintest amusement lifted the corners of his mouth. "But when you got home – you read it?"

"Yes."

"And so –?"

"That's why I'm here," she explained, with desperate simplicity. "Was it – was it true, what you put on that card?"

"That I never had any intention of buying authority over you? Yes, that was true."

"No, not that bit. I accept that now." She brushed it aside, for it had become unimportant. "The other bit. About – about –"

"Falling in love with your voice?" He completed the sentence for her with more consideration for her feelings than he usually showed. "Yes, of course. I fell in love with your voice the very first time I heard it. Immediately and irretrievably."

"With – my voice? Just – with my voice?"

There was an odd little silence. Then he laughed protestingly and asked, "What more do you want me to say? That I fell in love with *you* that first day?"

"Only if — it's true," she said breathlessly.

"It is not true," he replied coolly and categorically, and suddenly the world went cold and empty for her.

"Oh, I see." She put down her lashes and tried hard not to let any tears escape. But it had been a tremendously emotional and harrowing evening and her self-control was weak. In spite of all her efforts, two large tears spilled over and ran down her cheeks.

Then that beloved, half mocking voice said softly, "I think it took me two and a half weeks to fall in love with you yourself."

"You beast!" cried Anthea, and her lashes swept up, so that the tears could no longer be held back. "You beast! How dare you torment me like that!"

"I don't know," he said. And suddenly he was beside her and his uninjured arm was round her. "And I don't know how you can shed tears for me, my angry little beloved. I don't deserve it."

"No, you *don't* deserve it," she sobbed, burying her face against him.

"But I love you," he said softly, just above her head. "In my arrogant, imperfect, sometimes cruel way, I adore you. Are you listening to me?"

She nodded, her face still hidden.

"Well, listen well," he said, half teasingly, half tenderly, "because I shall probably never say all this to you again. I'm not in any way worthy of you. You are warm and basic and infinitely human, and that's why you are irresistible to a cold, self-contained creature like me. When I look at you it's like looking at the sunshine, and when I listen to you singing it's like hearing the music of the spheres. It was
186

utterly inevitable that I should love you. The miracle is that you should love me. If you marry me, you won't always be happy –"

"If I don't marry you, I shall never be entirely happy again," she said, looking up suddenly and speaking out of the depths of her profound conviction. "I know some of what you say of yourself is true, but I don't care. I know you'll make me shed many tears, but –"

"Not many, my darling," he said, and his lips were warm against hers. "I promise you that. And some of the weapons are in your hands now, you know. By admitting that I love you utterly, I've given you certain dominion over me."

"You're quite capable of taking it back, though, sometimes," she replied, with a flash of humour.

"No, he said, with absolute simplicity, "I can't. I may not be a generous or an easy giver. But what I give I never take back. Not my word, not my friendship, not my love."

"Have you ever given – your love before?" she asked timidly.

"Not to any woman."

She thought about Peroni, and for a moment she was tempted to mention her name. But suddenly the idea seemed unworthy. If he said he had not given his love to another woman, she believed him. The gossips could say what they pleased. Oscar Warrender's heart was hers.

The discovery was so breathtaking, so dazzling, that she gave a little gasp and flung her arms round his neck and kissed him over and over again. It was something she simply could not have imagined herself doing even an hour ago. Now it was the most completely right and natural thing in the world.

He gave a slight, incredulous laugh and returned her kisses, first with a tenderness which astounded her, and then with a passion which excited her more than anything else that had happened on that unbelievable evening.

Then, after a minute or two, he held her slightly away from him and said, with a wry little smile,

"And now, my darling, it's about time you went home to your safe, respectable boarding-house. You may be an angel, but I am not. I'll come down with you and get you a taxi, as I can't drive you home."

"No, you won't!" It was intoxicating to be able to contradict him with impunity. "You're not going to get your injured arm in and out of a coat sleeve again tonight. And I don't think," she added demurely, "that you'd better see me off in a dressing-gown at this hour of the night."

He laughed a little vexedly at that. But he said, "All right. The porter will get you a taxi." And then, almost as an afterthought, "When will you marry me?"

"Whenever you say."

"Perfect obedience still to the will of her operatic director, I'm glad to see," he said mockingly.

"No. Perfect agreement with the man I love," she retorted, and he put his hand against her cheek with a gesture of tenderness which made up for all the times he had been brutal to her.

"My little prima donna from the provinces," he said. "Well, we'll discuss a wedding date along with all the other aspects of your future tomorrow. It isn't going to be plain sailing, you know, being married to your conductor. There'll be plenty of spiteful people to say that you get on just because I favour you, for one thing."

"And will you favour me?" She looked up at him and smiled mischievously.

"On the contrary." He kissed her smiling mouth deliberately. "I shall probably be as hard on you as on myself, which is saying something. But remember, however harsh I am with you, I love you."

"And, however temperamental I am with you, I love you," she replied, which seemed to amuse him greatly.

He came with her to the door of the flat and rang the bell to summon the lift. Then as the lift slid smoothly upwards and the door opened, he said,

"From tomorrow onwards you will probably be offered the world. But it will be a year or two before you have earned the right to accept it. I hope the long wait will not be too irksome if we are together."

"It will be all too short," she assured him, with a smile, as she stepped into the lift. "Do you want me for a lesson tomorrow morning as usual?"

"No, darling, it will be Sunday," he reminded her. "To-morrow we'll relax – and see each other without a lesson. But on Monday" – suddenly his voice took on the familiar stern note – "I shall expect you at eleven. Don't be late. There's a lot of work to be done on that second act yet."

"Yes, Mr. Warrender," said Anthea. Then the lift door closed, and she was borne downwards.

Mills & Boon Classics

The very best of Mills & Boon
romances, brought back for those of you
who missed reading them when they
were first published.

There are three other Classics for you to collect this
April

CINDERELLA IN MINK
by Roberta Leigh
Nicola Rosten was used to the flattery and deference
accorded to a very wealthy woman. Yet Barnaby Grayson
mistook her for a down-and-out and set her to work in the
kitchen!

MASTER OF SARAMANCA
by Mary Wibberley
Gavin Grant was arrogant and overbearing, thought Jane, and
she hadn't ever disliked anyone quite so much. Yet . . .

NO GENTLE POSSESSION
by Anne Mather
After seven years, Alexis Whitney was returning to Karen's
small town. It was possible that he might not even remember
her — but Karen hoped desperately that he did.

If you have difficulty in obtaining any of these books through
your local paperback retailer, write to:

Mills & Boon Reader Service
P.O. Box 236, Thornton Road, Croydon, Surrey, CR9 3RU.

Mills & Boon Classics

The very best of Mills & Boon
romances, brought back for those of
you who missed reading them
when they were first published.

In
May
we bring back the following four
great romantic titles.

A MAN APART
by Jane Donnelly

Everyone who knew Libby Mason hoped that she and Ian
Blaney would make a match of it, and they were all quick to
point out how misguided she would be to entertain any
romantic ideas about the 'outsider' Adam Roscoe. But wasn't
it just possible that 'everyone' might be wrong?

RAPTURE OF THE DESERT
by Violet Winspear

Chrys didn't trust men, and Anton de Casenove was just the
type of man she most needed to be on her guard against — half
Russian prince, half man of the desert; a romantic combina-
tion. Could even Chrys be proof against it?

CHASE A GREEN SHADOW
by Anne Mather

Tamsyn had no doubt about her feeling for Hywel Benedict,
and it was equally clear that she affected him in some way —
but marriage? No, he said. He was too old for her. And there
were — other complications.

THE CRESCENT MOON
by Elizabeth Hunter

When Madeleine was stranded in Istanbul, there was no one to
whom she could turn for help except the lordly Maruk Bey,
who had told her that he found her 'dark, mysterious, and
very, very beautiful.' Could Madeleine trust such a man to aid
her?